Elizabeth K

The House Opposite

Elizabeth Kent

The House Opposite

1st Edition | ISBN: 978-3-75233-492-0

Place of Publication: Frankfurt am Main, Germany

Year of Publication: 2020

Outlook Verlag GmbH, Germany.

The
House

Opposite

A Mystery

By
Elizabeth Kent

CHAPTER I

WHAT I am about to relate occurred but a few years ago—in the summer of '99, in fact. You may remember that the heat that year was something fearful. Even old New Yorkers, inured by the sufferings of many summers, were overcome by it, and everyone who could, fled from the city. On the particular August day when this story begins, the temperature had been even more unbearable than usual, and approaching night brought no perceptible relief. After dining with Burton (a young doctor like myself), we spent the evening wandering about town trying to discover a cool spot.

At last, thoroughly exhausted by our vain search, I decided to turn in, hoping to sleep from sheer fatigue; but one glance at my stuffy little bedroom discouraged me. Dragging a divan before the window of the front room, I composed myself for the night with what resignation I could muster.

I found, however, that the light and noise from the street kept me awake; so, giving up sleep as a bad job, I decided to try my luck on the roof. Arming myself with a rug and a pipe, I stole softly upstairs. It was a beautiful starlight night, and after spreading my rug against a chimney and lighting my pipe I concluded that things really might be worse.

Across the street loomed the great Rosemere apartment-house, and I noted with surprise that, notwithstanding the lateness of the hour and of the season, several lights were still burning there. From two windows directly opposite, and on a level with me, light filtered dimly through lowered shades, and I wondered what possible motive people could have for shutting out the little air there was on such a night. My neighbours must be uncommonly suspicious, I thought, to fear observation from so unlikely a place as my roof; and yet that was the only spot from which they could by any chance be overlooked.

The only other light in the building shone clear and unobstructed through the open windows of the corresponding room two floors higher up. I was too far below to be able to look into this room, but I caught a suggestion of sumptuous satin hangings and could distinguish the tops of heavy gilt frames and of some flowering plants and palms.

As I sat idly looking upwards at these latter windows, my attention was suddenly arrested by the violent movement of one of the lace curtains. It was rolled into a cord by some unseen person who was presumably on the floor, and then dragged across the window. A dark object, which I took to be a human head, moved up and down among the palms, one of which fell with an audible crash. At the same moment I heard a woman's voice raised in a cry of terror. I leaped to my feet in great excitement, but nothing further occurred.

After a minute or so the curtain fell back into its accustomed folds, and I distinctly saw a man moving swiftly away from the window supporting on his shoulder a fair-haired woman. Soon afterwards the lights in this room were extinguished, to be followed almost immediately by the illumination of the floor above.

What I had just seen and heard would not have surprised me in a tenement, but that such scenes could take place in a respectable house like the Rosemere, inhabited largely by fashionable people, was indeed startling. Who could the couple be? And what could have happened? Had the man, coming home drunk, proceeded to beat the woman and been partially sobered by her cry; or was the woman subject to hysteria, or even insane? I remembered that the apartments were what are commonly known as double-deckers. That is to say: each one contained two floors, connected by a private staircase—the living rooms below, the bedrooms above. So I concluded, from seeing a light in what was in all probability a bedroom, that the struggle, or whatever the commotion had been, was over, and that the victim and her assailant, or perhaps the patient and her nurse, had gone quietly, and I trusted amicably, to bed.

Still ruminating over these different conjectures, I heard a neighbouring clock strike two. I now noticed for the first time signs of life in the lower apartment which I first mentioned; shadows, reflected on the blinds, moved swiftly to and fro, and, growing gigantic, vanished.

But not for long. Soon they reappeared, and the shades were at last drawn up. I had now an unobstructed view of the room, which proved to be a drawing-room, as I had already surmised. It was dismantled for the summer, and the pictures and furniture were hidden under brown holland. A man leant against the window with his head bowed down, in an attitude expressive of complete exhaustion or of great grief. It was too dark for me to distinguish his features; but I noticed that he was tall and dark, with a youthful, athletic figure.

After standing there a few minutes, he turned away. His actions now struck me as most singular. He crawled on the floor, disappeared under sofas, and finally moved even the heavy pieces of furniture from their places. However valuable the thing which he had evidently lost might be, yet 2 A.M. seemed hardly the hour in which to undertake a search for it.

Meanwhile, my attention had been a good deal distracted from the man by observing a woman in one of the bedrooms of the floor immediately above, and consequently belonging to the same suite. When I first caught sight of her, the room was already ablaze with light and she was standing by the window, gazing out into the darkness. At last, as if overcome by her emotions, she threw up her hands in a gesture of despair, and, kneeling down with her elbows on the window sill, buried her head in her arms. Her hair was so dark that, as she knelt there against the light, it was undistinguishable from her black dress.

I don't know how long she stayed in this position, but the man below had given up his search and turned out the lights long before she moved. Finally, she rose slowly up, a tall black-robed figure, and disappeared into the back of the room. I waited for some time hoping to see her again, but as she remained invisible and nothing further happened, and the approaching dawn held out hopes of a more bearable temperature below, I decided to return to my divan; but the last thing I saw before descending was that solitary light, keeping its silent vigil in the great black building.

CHAPTER II

I AM INVOLVED IN THE CASE

I T seemed to me that I had only just got to sleep on my divan when I was awakened by a heavy truck lumbering by. The sun was already high in the heavens, but on consulting my watch I found that it was only ten minutes past six. Annoyed at having waked up so early I was just dozing off again when my sleepy eyes saw the side door leading to the back stairs of the Rosemere slowly open and a young man come out.

Now I do not doubt that, except for what I had seen and heard the night before, I should not have given the fellow a thought; but the house opposite had now become for me a very hotbed of mystery, and everything connected with it aroused my curiosity. So I watched the young man keenly, although he appeared to be nothing but a grocer's or baker's boy going on his morning rounds. But looking at him again I thought him rather old for an errand boy, for they are seldom over eighteen, while this young fellow was twenty-five at the very least. He was tall, dark, and clean-shaven, although not very recently so. He wore no collar, and had on a short, black coat over which was tied a not immaculate white apron. On his arm hung a covered basket, which, from the way he carried it, I judged to be empty, or nearly so.

It may have been my imagination,—in fact, I am inclined to think it was,— but it certainly seemed to me that he stole furtively from the house and glanced apprehensively up and down the street, casting a look in my direction. I thought that he started on encountering my eyes. Be that as it may, he certainly drew his battered hat farther over his face, and, with both hands in his pockets, and chewing a straw with real or assumed carelessness, walked rapidly up town.

I now found my position by the window too noisy, so sought the quiet and darkness of my bedroom, where I fell immediately into such a heavy sleep that it was some time before I realised that the alarm-bell that had been clanging intermittently through my dreams was in reality my office-bell. Hurriedly throwing on a few clothes, I hastened to open the door.

A negro lad stood there, literally grey with terror. His great eyes rolled alarmingly in their sockets, and it was several minutes before I could make out that somebody had been killed, and that my services were required immediately.

5

Hastily completing my dressing, and snatching up my instrument case, I was ready to follow him in a few moments. What was my astonishment and horror when he led me to the Rosemere!

For a moment my heart stood still. My thoughts flew back to last night. So this was the explanation of that scream, and I had remained silent! Dolt, imbecile that I was! I felt positively guilty.

The large entrance hall through which I hurried was crowded with excited people, and, as I flew up in the elevator, I tried to prepare myself for the sight of a fair-haired girl weltering in her blood. On the landing at which we stopped were several workmen, huddled together in a small knot, with white, scared faces. One of the two doors which now confronted me stood open, and I was surprised to notice that it led, not to either of the apartments I had watched the night before, but to one of those on the farther side of the building. Yet here, evidently, was the corpse.

Passing through the small hall, filled with rolls of paper and pots of paints, I entered a room immediately on my right. Here several men stood together, gazing down at some object on the floor; but at my approach they moved aside and disclosed—not a golden-haired woman, as I had feared, but the body of a large man stretched out in a corner.

I was so astonished that I could not help giving vent to an exclamation of surprise.

"Do you know the gentleman?" inquired a man, whom I afterwards discovered to be the foreman of the workmen, with quick suspicion.

"No, indeed," I answered, as I knelt down beside the body.

A policeman stepped forward.

"Please, sir, don't disturb the corpse; the Coroner and the gen'l'man from headquarters must see him just as he is."

I nodded assent. One glance was sufficient to show me that life had been extinct for some time. The eyes were half open, staring stupidly before them. The mouth had fallen apart, disclosing even, white teeth. As he lay there on his back, with arms spread out, and his hands unclenched, his whole attitude suggested nothing so much as a drunken stupor. He appeared to be twenty-five or thirty years old. No wound or mark of violence was visible. He wore a short, pointed beard, and was dressed in a white linen shirt, a pair of evening trousers, a black satin tie, silk socks, and patent-leather pumps. By his side lay a Tuxedo coat and a low waistcoat. All his clothes were of fine texture, but somewhat the worse for wear. On the other hand, the pearl studs in his shirt-bosom were very handsome, and on his gold sleeve-links a crest was engraved.

As I said before, a glance had been enough to tell me that the man was dead; but I was astonished to discover, on examining him more closely, that he had been dead at least twenty-four hours; mortification had already set in.

As I arose to my feet, I noticed a small, red-haired man, in the most comical deshabille, regarding me with breathless anxiety.

"Well, Doc, what is it?"

"Of course, I can give no definite opinion without making a further examination," I said, "but I am inclined to believe that our friend succumbed to alcoholism or apoplexy; he has been dead twenty-four hours, and probably somewhat longer."

"There, now," exclaimed the foreman; "I knew he hadn't died last night; no, nor yistidy, neither."

"But it can't be, I tell you!" almost shrieked the little Irishman. "Where could he have come from? Oh, Lord," he wailed, "to think that sich a thing should have happened in this building! We only take the most iligant people; yes, sir, and now they'll lave shure, see if they don't. It'll give the house a bad name; and me as worked so hard to keep it genteel."

A commotion on the landing announced the arrival of a stout, florid individual, who turned out to be the Coroner, and a quiet, middle-aged man in plain clothes, whom I inferred, from the respect with which he was treated, to be no other than the "gen'l'man" from headquarters. After looking at the corpse for some moments, the Coroner turned to us and demanded:

"Who is this man?"

The little Irishman stepped forward. "We don't none of us know, sor."

"How came he here then?"

"The Lord only knows!"

"What do you mean?"

"Well, sor, it's this way. This apartment is being re-fixed, and five men were working here till six o'clock yistidy evening, and when they left they locks the door, and it has a Yale lock; and they brought me the key and I locks it away at once; and this morning at seven they come while I was still half asleep, having slept bad on account of the heat, and I gets up and opens the safe myself and takes out the key and gives it to this gintleman," pointing to the foreman; "and he come up here, and a few minutes afterwards I hear a great hue and cry and the workmen and elevaytor-boy come ashrieking that a body's murthered upstairs. How the fellow got in here, unless the Divil brought him, I can't think; and now here's the doctor that says he's been dead twenty-four hours!"

At my mention the Coroner turned towards me with a slight bow. "You are a doctor?"

"Yes, I am Dr. Charles Fortescue, of Madison Avenue. My office is exactly opposite; I was summoned this morning to see the corpse; I find that the man has been dead at least twenty-four hours. I have not yet made an examination of the body, as I did not wish to disturb it till you"—with a bow which included his companion—"had seen it; but I am inclined to think he died of alcoholism or apoplexy."

"Let me make you acquainted with Mr. Merritt, Dr. Fortescue," said the Coroner, waving his hand in the direction of the gentleman referred to. I was surprised to learn that this insignificant-looking person was really the famous detective.

"Now, gentlemen," said Mr. Merritt, "I must request you all to leave the room while Dr. Fortescue and I take a look round."

As soon as we were alone, the detective knelt down and proceeded to examine the body with astonishing quickness and dexterity. Nothing escaped him; even the darns in the socks appeared worthy of his interest. When he had finished, he beckoned me to approach, and together we turned the body over. As I had discovered no sign of violence, I was about to tell him that, unless the autopsy disclosed poison, the man had certainly died from natural causes, when Mr. Merritt pointed to a small drop of blood at the side of his shirt front immediately above the heart, which had escaped my observation. In the middle of this tiny spot a puncture was visible.

We now partially disrobed the corpse, and I was stupified to find that the deceased had indeed been assassinated, and by an instrument no larger than a knitting-needle. In the meantime, the detective had been carefully inspecting the clothing. There were no marks on anything except those with which laundries insist on disfiguring our linen. In the waistcoat pocket he found six dollars in bills and seventy-five cents in change; also a knife; but no watch, card, or letter.

Mr. Merritt now whipped out a magnifying glass and searched everything anew; but if he discovered any clue he kept the knowledge of it discreetly to himself. After going over every inch of the floor and examining the window he peered out.

"So you live there, Doctor," he remarked, with a glance opposite.

"No," I replied, "my house is further north; my office faces the other set of apartments."

Being curious to see if we were anywhere near either of the apartments I had watched during the night, I, too, leaned out and looked hastily in the direction of my roof. We were exactly on a level with it, and consequently the adjoining suite must be the one in which I had noticed the dark-haired woman and the man whose ill-timed hunt had puzzled me so much. Their behavior had certainly been very peculiar. Had they anything to do with this murder, I wondered. I was startled by a soft voice at my elbow, remarking quietly: "You seem struck by something." As I was not anxious, at least not yet, to tell him of my experiences of the night before, I tried to say in the most natural tone in the world: "Oh, I was only noticing that we are exactly on a level with my roof." "I had already observed that," he said. After a slight pause, he continued: "We must now find out who saw the deceased enter the building, for in a place so guarded by bell-boys, elevator-boys and night-watchmen as this is, it seems hardly possible that he could have come in unperceived."

On entering the next room we found the Coroner deep in conversation with the foreman. He turned abruptly to me:

"This man tells me that you uttered an exclamation of surprise on seeing the corpse. What made you do so?"

That unlucky ejaculation! I hesitated a moment, rather at a loss to know what to reply. Every one turned towards me, and I felt myself actually blushing. "I was at first struck by a fancied resemblance," I at last managed to stammer, "but on looking closer I saw I had been completely mistaken."

"Humph," grunted the Coroner, and I was aware that every one in the room eyed me with suspicion. "Well," he continued, still looking at me severely, "can you tell us what the man died of?" "Yes," I answered; "he met his death by being stabbed to the heart by a very small weapon, possibly a stiletto, but a sharp knitting-needle, or even a hat pin, could have caused the wound. The crime was committed while he was unconscious, or at least semi-conscious, either from some drug or alcohol; or he may have been asleep. He made no resistance, and in all probability never knew he had been hurt."

There was profound silence.

"It is, then, impossible that this wound was self-inflicted," inquired the Coroner.

"Quite impossible," I rejoined.

"So that he was presumably murdered the night before last and smuggled into this apartment some time between six o'clock last evening and seven o'clock this morning?" continued the Coroner. Then, turning to the little red-headed manager, he asked:

"Now, Mr. McGorry, how is it possible for this corpse to have been brought here? The foreman testifies that he himself locked the door in the presence of several workmen; you tell me that the key remained in your safe all night. Now, please explain how this body got here?"

"Lord-a-mercy, sor, you don't think as I did it!" shrieked McGorry. "Why, sor, I never saw the man before in my life; besides, I have got a alibi, sor; yes, sor, a alibi."

"Stop, Mr. McGorry; don't get so excited; nobody is accusing you of anything. But if this place was locked up last night, how came the body here this morning? The lock has not been tampered with. Was there a duplicate key?"

"Yis, sor; but the other key was also in my safe," replied McGorry.

"Have either of these keys ever been missing?"

"Shure and they haven't been out of my keeping since the apartment was vacated last May, until three days ago when the painters begun work here. Since then they have had one of the keys during the day, but have always returned it before leaving."

"Now, tell me," continued the Coroner, turning to the foreman, "has the key been missing since you had it?"

"Not that I know of; we leave it sticking in the door all day, and only take it out when we leave."

"So that it is possible that a person might have come to the door, taken the key, and kept it for some hours without your noticing it?"

"Yes, sir, it's possible, but it aint likely; I haven't seen anyone pass since I've been working here."

"Could the corpse have been brought in here any other way than through the front door?"

"No, Mr. Coroner," a quiet voice at my side replied; "I have just examined the fire-escape and all the windows. The fastenings have not been tampered with, and the dust on the fire-escape shows no signs of recent disturbance." Mr. Merritt had gone on his search so unobtrusively that I had not noticed his absence till he reappeared, a good deal less immaculate than before.

"Is it possible to enter this building unperceived?" the Coroner resumed.

"I should have said not," replied McGorry; "but now everything seems possible." Even the Coroner had to smile at his despondent tone.

"The front door is opened at seven o'clock and closed at eleven, unless there's something special going on," McGorry continued, "and during those hours there are always one or two boys in the hall, and often three. After eleven the watchman opens the front door and takes the people up in the elevaytor. No one but meself has the key to this outside door."

"Does the watchman never leave the front hall except to take people up in the elevator?"

"Well, I don't say niver, sor, but he's niver far off."

"Then I gather that it would be just possible for a person to get out of this house unperceived between eleven P.M. and seven A.M., but impossible, or nearly so, for him to enter?"

"Yes, that's so, that's what I think, sor."

"Well, what about the back door?" I asked.

"Well, the back door is opened at six and closed at tin," replied McGorry.

"The back door is not guarded during the day, is it?" I went on, forgetting the Coroner in my eagerness.

"Doctor," broke in the latter, "allow me to conduct this inquiry. Yes, McGorry, who watches over that?"

"Well, sor, at present no one; there's a back elevaytor, but it don't run in summer, as the house is almost empty."

"Then, as I understand it, any one can enter or leave the building by the back stairs, at any time during the day, unseen, or at any rate unnoticed; but after ten o'clock they would require the assistance of some one in the house to let them in?"

"That's so, sor."

"Now, you are sure that the deceased was not a temporary inmate of this building; that he wasn't staying with any of the parties who are still here?"

"Certain, sor."

"And no one has the slightest clue to his identity?"

"No one has seen him except these gen'l'men and Jim. He's the elevaytor boy who went for you, Doc, and he didn't say nothing about knowing him."

The Coroner paused a moment.

"What families have you at present in the building?"

"Well, sor, most of our people are out of town, having houses at Newport, or Lenox, and thereabouts," McGorry answered, with a vague sweep of his hand, which seemed to include all those favored regions which lie so close together in fashionable geography. "Just now there are only two parties in the house."

"Yes, and who are they?"

"Well, sor, there's Mr. C. H. Stuart, who occupies the ground floor right; and Mr. and Mrs. Atkins, who have the apartments above this, only at the other end of the building." I pricked up my ears. Atkins, then, must be the name of the golden-haired lady and her assailant.

"Have these people been here long?"

"Mr. Stuart has been with us seven years. He is a bachelor. Mr. and Mrs. Atkins have only been here since May; they are a newly-married couple, I am told." And not a word of the mysterious pair I had seen in the adjoining apartment! Was McGorry holding something back, or was he really ignorant of their presence in the building?

"Are you sure, Mr. McGorry, that there is no one else in the house?" I interrupted again.

"Yes, sor." Then a light broke over his face: "No, sor; you are quite right" (I hadn't said anything). "Miss Derwent has been two nights here, but she's off again this morning." Mr. Merritt here whispered something to the Coroner, whereupon the latter turned to McGorry and said: "Please see that no one leaves this building till I have seen them. I don't wish them to be told that a murder has been committed, unless they have heard it already, which is most probable. Just inform them that there has been an accident, do you hear?"

"Oh, Mr. Coroner," exclaimed McGorry, turning almost as red as his hair in his excitement; "shure and you wouldn't mix Miss Derwent up in this! Lord, she ain't used to such scenes; she'd faint, and then her mother would never forgive me!"

"Every one, Miss Derwent included, must view the corpse," he replied, sternly.

"Oh, sor, but——"

"Silence!" thundered the Coroner; "the law must be obeyed."

So the manager went reluctantly out to give the desired order. On his return, the Coroner resumed:

"Who is Miss Derwent?"

"Why Miss May Derwent," exclaimed McGorry; "she's just Miss May Derwent." So it was the fashionable beauty I had been watching so far into the night. Strange, and stranger!

"Miss May Derwent," McGorry continued, taking pity on our ignorance, "is the only daughter of Mrs. Mortimer Derwent. She arrived here unexpectedly on Tuesday. She had missed her train, she said, and came here to pass the night."

"Did she come alone?"

"Yis, sor."

"Without even a maid?"

"Yis, sor."

"Surely that is an unusual thing for a rich young lady to do?"

"Yis, sor," replied McGorry, apologetically; "she has never done it before. Maybe the maid was taken on by the train."

"Did Miss Derwent bring any luggage?"

"Nothing but a hand-bag, sor."

"And yet she stayed two nights! Do you know any reason for her staying here so long?"

"No, sor, unless it was she had some shopping to do. A good many parcels come for her yistidy afternoon."

"Have you a key to her apartment?"

"Yis, sor; when families goes away for the summer they leaves one key with me and takes the other with them."

"Did you let Miss Derwent into her apartment, or did she have the key?"

"I let her in."

"Did anyone wait on the young lady while she was here?"

"What do you mean by that?" inquired McGorry, cautiously.

"Why, did anyone go into her place to get her meals and tidy up, etc?"

"No, sor, not that I know of."

"Doesn't it strike you as peculiar that a young lady, reared in the lap of luxury and unaccustomed to doing the least thing for herself should go to an apartment in which dust and dirt had been accumulating for several months and voluntarily spend two nights there, without even a servant to perform the necessary chores for her, mind you?"

"She went out for her meals," McGorry put in, anxiously, "and young ladies, especially the rich ones, think roughing it a lark."

There was a slight pause.

"What servants are there in the building besides your employees, Mr. McGorry?"

"Mr. Stuart, he keeps a man and his wife—French people they are; and Mrs. Atkins, she keeps two girls."

The Coroner now rose, and, followed by Mr. Merritt, proceeded towards the room where the dead man lay.

"Send up your employees, one by one, McGorry."

"Yis, sor."

On the threshold the detective paused a moment, and to my astonishment and delight requested me to accompany them. The Coroner frowned, evidently considering me a very unnecessary addition to the party, but his displeasure made no difference to me; I was only too happy to be given this opportunity of watching the drama unfold itself.

CHAPTER III

W E took our places at the foot of the corpse, with our backs to the light and silently awaited developments. In a few minutes McGorry returned, followed by the electrician, and during the rest of the time remained in the room checking off the men as they came in. It is needless for me to repeat all the testimony, as a great deal of it was perfectly irrelevant; suffice it to say that the electrician, engineer, and janitress all passed the ordeal without adding an iota to our information. The watchman when called persisted, after the severest cross-questioning, in his first assertion that neither on Wednesday night nor last night had he seen or heard anything suspicious. The only person he had admitted on either night was Mr. Atkins, who had returned at about half-past one that very morning; he was sure that he had seen no stranger leave the building.

At last Jim, the elevator boy, was called in. He appeared still very much frightened, and only looked at the corpse with the greatest reluctance.

"Have you ever seen this man before?" demanded the Coroner.

"No, sah," answered Jim, in a shaking voice.

"Now, my lad, take another look at him. Are you still so sure that you have never seen him before," gently insisted Mr. Merritt; "for, you see, we have reason to believe that you have." Jim began to tremble violently, as he cast another glance at the dead man.

"Lord-a-massy, sah; p'raps I did, p'raps I did; I dunno, he looks some like —not 'zactly——"

"Do you know his name?"

"No, sah."

"When did you see him last?"

"Tuesday ebenin', sah." Here the boy glanced apprehensively at McGorry.

"Come, come, my lad," the Coroner exclaimed, impatiently; "tell us all you know about the man. The truth, now, and the whole truth, mind you; and don't you look at any one to see how they are going to like what you say, either."

"No, sah." Jim hesitated a moment, then burst out: "I do think as he's the same gem'man as come to see Miss Derwent last winter, and he come to call

15

on her about half-past six on Tuesday."

"Miss Derwent—" exclaimed McGorry, taking a step forward.

"McGorry," said the Coroner, severely, "don't try to interfere with justice and intimidate witnesses. Now, my boy, tell us how long did the gentleman stay with Miss Derwent."

"Dey went out togedder 'most immedjutely, and den dey come back togedder."

"At what time did they return?"

"Must have been 'bout eight, sah."

"Did he go upstairs with the young lady?"

"Yes, sah."

"When did he leave?"

"I can't say, sah; I didn't see him leave."

"How was that?"

"Well, you see, sah, in de summer, when de house is mos' empty, we's not so partic'lar as we are in de winter, and we takes turn and turn about oftener, 'specially in de ebenin'."

"I see," said the Coroner.

"An' so dat ebenin I goes off at half-past eight and Joe he run de elevator till eleben."

"Did any one call on Miss Derwent yesterday?"

"I see nobody, sah."

"Did the young lady go out during the day?"

"Yes, sah."

"Tell us all you know of her movements."

Jim rubbed his woolly pate in some perplexity: "Well, sah, yesterday de young lady she went out mighty early, little before eight, maybe, and den she come back about ten; but she don't stay long; goes out again mos' right away."

Here Jim paused, evidently searching his memory.

"'Pears to me she come in 'bout half-past twelve; at any rate 'twasn't no later, and she goes out again immedjutely. Yes, sah, and den I seed her come in 'bout seven, and I aint seen her again," he ended up with a sigh of relief.

"And you are sure that she was alone each time you saw her?"

"Yes, sah. A good many parcels come for her in de afternoon," he added.

"Well, Jim," said the Coroner, "you may go now; but mind you, don't say a word about this business to any one; do you hear? If I find out you have been gossiping I'll know how to deal with you," and he looked so threatening that I'm sure the unfortunate boy expected capital punishment to follow any incautious remark.

"Pardon me," said Mr. Merritt, with a slight bow towards the Coroner, "but I should like to ask Jim how this man was dressed when he saw him last."

"Just so 's he is now, sah," replied Jim, pointing to the Tuxedo coat, which had been thrown over the body.

The negro lad who next appeared, bowing and scraping, was not at all intimidated by the scene before him, and seemed to think himself quite the hero of the occasion.

"Your name is Joe Burr, I believe," began the Coroner, consulting a small paper he held in his hand, "and you run the elevator here?"

"Yes, sah."

"Now look carefully at this body and tell me if you recognize it as that of anyone you know."

The boy looked at the dead man attentively for some moments and then answered: "Yes, sah."

"Who is he?"

"I dunno his name, sah; he wouldn't send up his card."

"Have you seen him often?"

"No, sah; just dat once."

"When was that?"

"Tuesday ebenin', sah."

"At what time?"

"It was a quarter to ten, 'zactly."

"How are you so sure of the exact time?" the Coroner asked, in some surprise.

"'Cause I thought it mighty late to call on a lady, and so I looked at de clock when I come down."

"Do you remember his ever calling on Miss Derwent before?"

"Why, sah, 'twasn't Miss Derwent he was calling on; 'twas Mrs. Atkins." This was a surprise; even the detective seemed interested.

"So it was Mrs. Atkins he had been calling on," exclaimed the Coroner.

"No, sah; it were Mrs. Atkins he gwine ter call on. He only come at a quarter to ten. He wouldn't send up his card; said he's 'spected."

"And did Mrs. Atkins receive him?"

"Yes, sah."

"Do you remember at what time he left?"

"No, sah; I didn't see him go out."

"Now, Joe, there was another gentleman calling in the building on that evening. When did he leave?"

Joe seemed bewildered. "I didn't see no other gem'man, sah."

"Now, my lad, try and remember!"

"No, sah; I dun saw no one else. Mr. Stuart, he come in at ten———"

"No, no; it is a tall, dark gentleman, slightly resembling the corpse, that we want to hear about."

"I see no such party, sah."

"Didn't a gentleman answering to this description call here at about half-past six and ask for a lady?"

"I couldn't say, sah; I wa'n't in de building at dat time."

"Did you see Miss Derwent on Tuesday?"

"Yes, sah; I seen her arrive."

"Didn't you see her go out again?"

"No, sah."

"How long were you out?"

"I went out at six, sah, and stayed till eight, or maybe later."

"So you persist in saying that the only stranger you saw enter or leave the building on Tuesday evening, was the deceased?"

"Yes, sah."

"And you are quite sure that you are not mistaken in your identification?"

"Yes, sah; I noticed him partic'lar."

"What made you notice him particularly?"

The lad hesitated. "Out with it," said the Coroner.

"Well, sah, he seemed like he been drinking."

"How did he show it?"

"He talked loud and angry, sah."

"Do you know what he was angry about?"

"You see, sah, we have orders to ask visitors to send deir names, or deir cards up, and to wait in de reception room till we find out if de parties are at home, or will see dem. Well, he comes in and says very loud, gettin' into de elevator, 'Take me up to de fifth floor,' and I says, says I, 'Do you mean Mrs. Atkins?' and he says, 'Yes, fellow, and be quick 'bout it.' And den I asks him to wait, and send up his card, and he roars: 'Min' your own business, fellow; I'm 'spected.' So I gwine take him up, and rings de bell, and he says: 'Dat's all.' But I waited till de door opened, and there were Mrs. Atkins herself, and she didn't say not'in', and he jus' went in."

Joe paused for breath.

"Is Mrs. Atkins in the habit of answering the door-bell herself?"

"No, sah; I neber see her do so befo'."

"Was Mr. Atkins in the house at the time?"

"No, sah; de gem'man was out of town." Another sensation!

"When did he return?"

"Some time las' night."

"Now," inquired the Coroner, "what can you tell us about Miss Derwent's movements during the last two days?"

Joe's answers coincided, as far as they went, with Jim's statements.

"And Mrs. Atkins,—what did she do yesterday," the Coroner asked.

"Well, sah, she went out mighty early and stayed till late in de arternoon, and when she come in she had her veil all pulled down, but 'peared to me she had been crying."

"Did she say anything?"

"No, sah."

"Now, Joe, would it have been possible on Tuesday evening for a man to walk downstairs, and go out, without your seeing him, while you were running the elevator?"

"Yes, sah, p'raps," the lad answered, dubiously; "but Tony, he's de hallboy, he would 'a seen him."

"Have you told us all you know of the deceased?"

"Yes, sah."

"And you have not noticed any strangers hanging around the building during the last few days?"

"No, sah."

"Very well, then; you may go. Send in Tony."

"Yes, sah; t'ank you, sah," and Joe bowed himself out.

A few minutes later a small darky appeared.

"Now, Tony," began the Coroner, solemnly, "look at this man carefully; did you ever see him before?" The boy looked at the body attentively for some time, then said: "No, sah."

"Do you mean to say that you saw no one resembling the deceased come to this building on Tuesday evening?"

"No, sah."

"Where were you on that evening? Now, be careful what you answer."

"Well, sah, I went out 'bout half-past six to do some errands for Mr. McGorry." McGorry nodded assent to this.

"And when did you return?"

"Guess it must have been mos' eight, sah, but I disremember, 'zactly."

"Did you see Miss Derwent either come in or go out on Tuesday evening?"

"Yes, sah, I seen her come; she had a satchel."

"But did you see her again after that?"

"No, sah."

"Mrs. Atkins—what did she do on Tuesday?"

"Dunno, sah; didn't see her go out all day."

"And yesterday, what did she do then?"

"Mrs. Atkins? She went out in de mornin' and come in in de ebenin'."

"Did you notice anything unusual about her?"

"Well, 'peared to us she'd been crying."

"Can you remember who went in or out of the building on Tuesday evening?" the Coroner asked.

"Well, sah, near's I can say only two gem'men come in—Mr. Stuart, and a gem'man who called on Mrs. Atkins."

"Does the corpse at all resemble that gentleman?"

"I couldn't rightly say, sah."

"Why not?"

"Well, sah, I was a-sittin' in de office when he come, an' I jus' see a big man go past and heard him talkin' loud in de elevator."

"While Joe was upstairs what did you do?"

"I sat in de front hall, sah."

"Did you see anyone go out?"

"No, sah."

After being severely admonished not to speak of this affair to anyone, Tony was allowed to depart.

"Now we have got through with the employees of the building," said the Coroner, "and must begin on the families and their servants."

"Yes, Mr. Coroner, and I think I had better step up-stairs myself and tell Mr. and Mrs. Atkins that you want to see them," said Mr. Merritt, "and, in case the lady should be overcome by the sad news, perhaps it would be as well for Dr. Fortescue to come along also."

I was only too delighted, of course.

CHAPTER IV

UNWILLING WITNESSES

N OT waiting for the elevator, we walked up the intervening flight and rang a bell on our right. The door was opened by a neat-looking maid, who showed some surprise at our early call.

"Is Mr. Atkins at home?" inquired the detective.

"Yes, sir; but he is having his breakfast."

"Ah, indeed; I am sorry to disturb him," replied Mr. Merritt. "However, it can't be helped. Will you please tell your master that two gentlemen must see him for a few moments on important business."

"Yes, sir," and showing us into a gaudily furnished room on our left, the girl vanished. I saw at once that this was not the scene of last night's drama, but a smaller room adjoining the other. My observations were almost immediately interrupted by the entrance of a young man, whose handsome face was at that moment disfigured by a scowl.

"Mr. Atkins, I believe," said Mr. Merritt, advancing towards him with his most conciliatory smile. Mr. Atkins nodded curtly. "It is my painful duty," continued the detective, "to inform you that a very serious accident has occurred in the building."

The frown slowly faded from the young man's forehead, giving place to a look of concern. "Oh, I'm so sorry!" he exclaimed, in the most natural manner; "what has happened? Can I do anything?"

"Well, Mr. Atkins," replied Mr. Merritt, slowly, "to tell you the truth, a man has been killed, and as we haven't been able to find any one so far who can identify him we are going through the formality of asking every one in the building to take a look at the corpse, hoping to discover somebody who knew the dead man, or at any rate can give us some clue to his identity. Will you and Mrs. Atkins and your two servants, therefore, kindly step down-stairs? The body is lying in the unoccupied apartment on the next floor."

"Killed!" exclaimed young Atkins. "How dreadful! how did it happen?" But without waiting for an answer he pulled out his watch, which he consulted anxiously. "Pardon me, gentlemen, but I have a most important engagement down town which it is impossible for me to postpone. My wife is not up yet, and I really can't wait for her to get ready; but I can go with you now, and take a look at the poor fellow on my way out. In the meantime, Mrs. Atkins will dress as quickly as possible, and follow with the two girls as soon as she is ready."

"All right," said Mr. Merritt; "that will do nicely. Dr. Fortescue," with a wave of his hand in my direction, "will stay here, and escort Mrs. Atkins down-stairs. Ladies sometimes are overcome by the sight of death."

"Yes, yes; and my wife is very excitable," rejoined the young man. "I am glad Dr. Fortescue will wait and go down with her—if it isn't troubling you too much," he added, turning towards me.

"Not at all," I replied, politely but firmly, with my eyes on Mr. Merritt. "I shall be delighted to *return* for Mrs. Atkins in a quarter of an hour and escort her down-stairs."

I watched the detective keenly to see how he would take this disregarding of his orders, but he only smiled amiably, almost triumphantly, I thought. Mr. Atkins now left us, and I could hear him dashing up-stairs several steps at a time. How I longed to pierce the ceiling, and hear how he broke the news to his wife, and above all to observe how she took it. He returned in a few minutes, and, snatching his hat from the hall-table, prepared to follow us. On the way down he inquired with great interest about the accident, but Merritt put him off with evasive replies. When confronted with the dead body, he gazed at it calmly, but with a good deal of curiosity.

"Did you know the deceased?" the Coroner asked him.

The young man shook his head. "Never saw him before." Then, looking at the corpse more closely he exclaimed: "Why, he is a gentleman; can't you find out who he is?"

"We haven't been able to, so far," replied the Coroner.

"How did the accident occur?"

"He was murdered."

The young man started back in horror.—"Murdered, and in this house— How, when?"

"Presumably the night before last."

Was it my imagination, or did Mr. Atkins turn slightly pale? "Tuesday night," he muttered. After a brief silence he turned to us, and withdrawing his eyes from the corpse with obvious difficulty, said, in a hearty, matter-of-fact voice: "Gentlemen, I regret that I have to leave you. I should like to hear some more of this affair, but I suppose if you do discover anything you will keep it pretty close?"

"You bet we'll try to," the Coroner assured him. After shaking us all most cordially by the hand, Mr. Atkins departed, and was escorted down-stairs by the detective, whose excessive politeness seemed to me very suspicious. "Was he going to put a sleuth on the young man's tracks?" I wondered.

The air in the room was heavy with the odour of death, so I stepped out on the landing. The workmen were all talking in low tones. "I know that Frenchman did it; I know it," I overheard one of them say. Much excited by these words, I was just going to ask who the Frenchman was, and why he should be suspected, when Mr. Merritt stepped out of the elevator and rang the bell of the opposite apartment. Miss Derwent had evidently not been far off, for the door was opened almost immediately, and a tall, slight young figure stood on the threshold. She was dressed in a quiet travelling suit, and a thick brown veil pulled down over her face rendered her features, in the dim light of the landing, completely invisible.

"Miss Derwent?" inquired Mr. Merritt. She bowed. "You have no doubt been told," he continued, "that a very serious accident has occurred in the building." She inclined her head slowly. "As we have been unable to identify the corpse"—here the detective paused, but she gave no sign and he went on —"we are asking every one in the house to take a look at it."

Instead of answering, the girl went back into the apartment, but returned in a minute, carrying a handbag. Stepping out on to the landing she shut and locked the door behind her with apparent composure. As she turned to follow the detective she asked, in a low but distinct voice: "How did this accident occur?"

"That, we have not yet been able to ascertain," he replied, leading her to the room where the dead lay. I hastily stepped back and resumed my former position at the foot of the corpse. As the girl crossed the threshold she hesitated a moment, then walked steadily in.

"Miss May Derwent, I believe?" the Coroner inquired, in his suavest tones. Again she bowed assent.

"Please look at this man and tell me if you have ever seen him before." Before replying, the girl slowly lifted her veil and revealed to my astonished eyes, not only a face of very unusual beauty, but—and this is what I found inexplicable—coils of golden hair! Where were the raven locks I had seen only a few hours before? Had I dreamed them? But no, my memory was too clear on this point. My surprise was so great that I am afraid I showed it, for I caught Mr. Merritt looking at me with one of his enigmatical smiles. Miss Derwent was excessively pale, with heavy black rings under her eyes, but otherwise she seemed perfectly composed. She looked at the corpse a moment, then turning towards the Coroner, said, in a clear, steady voice: "I do not know the man."

"Have you ever seen him before?"

"No," she answered, quietly.

"Miss Derwent, pardon my questioning you still further, but I have been told that a gentleman closely resembling the deceased called on you on Tuesday evening. Now, do you see any resemblance between the two?"

A burning blush overspread the girl's face, and then she grew so ghastly pale that I moved to her side, fearing she would fall.

"Mr. Coroner, can't the rest of the questions you have to ask Miss Derwent be put to her somewhere else?" I suggested. "The atmosphere here is intolerable."

"Certainly," he replied, with unexpected mildness.

I drew the young lady's unresisting hand through my arm and supported her into the next room. She was trembling so violently that she would have fallen if I had not done so, and I could see that it was only by the greatest self-control that she kept any semblance of composure.

"Now," resumed the Coroner, "if you feel well enough, will you kindly answer my last question?"

"The gentleman who called on me on Tuesday does not resemble the dead man, except in so far that they both have black, pointed beards."

"At what time did your friend leave you on Tuesday evening?" was the next question asked.

"I cannot see why the private affairs of my visitors or myself should be pried into," she replied, haughtily. "I decline to answer."

"My dear young lady," here interposed Mr. Merritt, "you have, of course, every right not to answer any question that you think likely to incriminate you, but," he continued with a smile, "it is hardly possible that anything could do that. On the other hand, it is our duty to try and sift this matter to the bottom. You certainly will agree with the necessity of it when I tell you that this man has been murdered!"

"Murdered!" the girl repeated, as if dazed. "Oh, no!"

"I regret to say that there is absolutely no doubt of it. Now, one of the elevator boys has identified the corpse as that of the gentleman who called on you the day before yesterday. I do not doubt that he was mistaken,—in fact, I am sure of it; but as no one saw your friend leave the building, it becomes incumbent on us to make sure that he did so. It will save a great deal of trouble to us, and perhaps to yourself, if you will tell us the gentleman's name and at what hour he left here."

She had covered her face with her hands, but now dropped them, and lifting her head, faced us with an air of sudden resolution.

"Gentlemen," she began, then hesitated and looked at us each in turn, "you can readily imagine that it will be a terrible thing for me if my name should in any way, however indirectly, be connected with this tragedy. But I see that it is useless to refuse to answer your questions. It will only make you believe that I have something to conceal. I can but ask you, you on whom I have no claim, to shield from publicity a girl who has put herself in a terribly false position."

"Miss Derwent, I think I can assure you that we will do everything in our power to help you. Nothing you say here shall be heard beyond these walls unless the cause of justice demands it." The Coroner spoke with considerable warmth. Evidently, Miss May's charms had not been without their effect on him.

"Very well, then," said the girl, "I will answer your questions. What do you want to know?"

"In the first place, please tell us how you came to spend two nights in an unoccupied apartment?"

"I suppose you already know," she answered, a trifle bitterly, "that I arrived here unexpectedly on Tuesday afternoon?" The Coroner made a motion of assent.

"I had reached the city earlier in the day, and had meant to catch the five o'clock train to Bar Harbor. As I had several errands to do, I sent my maid ahead to the Grand Central Depot with orders to engage a stateroom and check my luggage. I forgot to notice how the time was passing till I caught sight of a clock in Madison Square pointing to eight minutes to five. I jumped into a hansom, but got to the station just in time to see the train steam away, with my maid hanging distractedly out of a window." She paused a moment. "A gentleman happened to be with me," she continued with downcast eyes, "so we consulted together as to what I had better do. On looking up the trains I found that I could not get back to my mother's country place till nine o'clock that evening, and then should have to leave home again at a frightfully early hour so as to catch the morning train to Bar Harbor. Otherwise I should be obliged to wait over till the following afternoon and take a long night journey by myself, which I knew my mother would not wish me to do. Altogether, it seemed so much simpler to remain in town if I could only find a place to go to. Suddenly, our apartment occurred to me. Of course, I knew that the world would not approve of my staying here alone; nevertheless, I decided to do so."

"You went out again very soon after your arrival, did you not?" asked the Coroner.

"Yes," she answered, "as there was no way of getting any food here, my friend" (she hesitated slightly over the last word) "had little difficulty in persuading me to dine with him at a quiet restaurant in the neighbourhood."

"Did the gentleman return to the Rosemere after dinner?"

"Yes."

"And did he leave you then?"

Miss Derwent hesitated a moment, then, throwing her head back she answered proudly: "No!" But a deep crimson again suffused her cheek, and she added almost apologetically: "It was all so unconventional that I did not see why I should draw the line at his spending the evening with me. He was a very intimate friend."

"Why do you use the past tense?" asked Mr. Merritt. She cast a little frightened glance in his direction, evidently startled at being caught up so quickly: "We—we had a very serious disagreement," she murmured.

"Was the disagreement so serious as to put an end to your friendship?" inquired the detective.

"Yes," she replied curtly, while an angry light came into her eyes.

"At what time did the gentleman leave you?" resumed the Coroner.

"It was very late;—after eleven, I think."

"And you have not seen him again since then?"

"Certainly not," she replied.

"Why did you not carry out your first intention of leaving the city on the following morning?"

The girl appeared slightly embarrassed as she answered: "I did not feel like paying visits just at the moment, and besides I had not enough money to carry me as far as Bar Harbor. My maid had most of my money, and I was no longer willing to borrow from my visitor, as I had intended doing."

"Excuse my questioning you still further," said the Coroner, with a glance of admiration at the beautiful girl, who was fretting under the examination, "but, why, then, didn't you return to your home?"

"I did not wish to do so." Then, catching Mr. Merritt's eye, she added: "I had been a good deal upset by—by what had occurred the night before and felt the need of a day to myself. Besides, I had some shopping to do, and thought this a good opportunity to do it. I am going home this morning."

"Thank you, Miss Derwent," exclaimed the Coroner, heartily; "your explanations are perfectly satisfactory. Only you have forgotten to tell us the gentleman's name."

"Why need you know his name?" she demanded, passionately, "you will soon find out who this unknown man is. There must be hundreds of people in this city who knew him. Why should I tell you the name of my visitor? I refuse to do so."

"Miss Derwent is quite right," interposed the detective, with unexpected decision; "once convinced that the dead man and her friend are not identical, and the latter's name ceases to be of any importance to us."

"Quite so, quite so," the Coroner rather grudgingly assented.

"Can I go now?" she inquired.

"Certainly," said the Coroner, cordially. "Good-day, Miss."

I was just going to offer myself as an escort when Mr. Merritt stepped quietly forward, and possessed himself of the young lady's bag. With a distant bow, that included impartially the Coroner and myself, Miss Derwent left the room.

"Remember Mrs. Atkins," the detective murmured as he prepared to follow her. I nodded a curt assent. My brain was in a whirl. What was I to believe? This beautiful, queenlike creature seemed incapable of deceit, and yet—who were the two people I had so lately seen in her apartment? Why had no mention been made of them? No matter; I felt my belief in the young girl's innocence and goodness rise superior to mere facts, and then and there vowed to become her champion should she ever need one, which I very much feared she might. I was vaguely annoyed that the detective should have insisted on escorting her. Had he a motive for this, I wondered, or had he simply succumbed to her fascination, like the rest of us? At any rate, I didn't like it, and I rang Mrs. Atkins's bell in considerable ill humour.

CHAPTER V

"**I** S Mrs. Atkins ready?" I inquired of the pretty maid. Before she had time to answer, I heard the frou-frou of silk skirts advancing rapidly towards me. The perfume I had already noticed grew still more overpowering, and the lady herself appeared. And an exceedingly pretty little woman she proved to to be, too, with golden hair and cheeks that rivalled the roses. Her large blue eyes were as innocent and, it would be hypercritical to add, as expressionless as her sisters' of the toy-shop. A white muslin garment, slashed in every direction to admit of bands and frills of lace, enveloped her small person, and yards of blue ribbon floated around her. Her tiny, dimpled fingers were covered with glittering rings, which, however, scarcely outshone her small pink nails. She beamed coquettishly at me, showing some very pretty, sharp little teeth as she did so, and I found myself smiling back at her, completely forgetting the tragic errand I had come on.

"Oh, Doctor," she cried, in a high treble voice, "isn't it dreadful! They tell me that a poor man has been killed in the building, and I am so terrified at having to look at him! Must I really do so?" She wrung her hands in graceful distress.

"I'm afraid you must," I replied, smiling down at her.

"But you will go with me, won't you?" she begged.

"Certainly, dear Madam, and if your servants are also ready we had better get it over immediately."

As the lady crossed the threshold of her apartment she tucked her hand confidingly into my arm, as if the support of the nearest man were her indisputable right, and, followed by the two servants, we proceeded in this fashion down-stairs. Mr. Merritt met us on the landing, and, signing to the two girls to wait outside, ushered us into the room where the body lay.

As Mrs. Atkins caught sight of the dead man a great shudder shook her whole body, and I felt the hand on my arm grow suddenly rigid. She neither screamed nor fainted, but stood strangely still, as if turned to stone, her eyes riveted on the corpse in a horrified stare.

"Mrs. Atkins?" inquired the Coroner.

She seemed incapable of answering him.

"Mrs. Atkins," he repeated, a little louder, "do you recognise the deceased?"

This time she moved slightly and tried to moisten her grey lips. At last, with a visible effort, she slowly raised her eyes and glanced about her with fear.

"No, no," she murmured, in a hollow voice.

"Mrs. Atkins, I must request you to look at the dead man again," the detective said, fixing his eyes on her. "One of the elevator boys has identified the body as that of a gentleman who called on you on Tuesday evening."

She raised her arm as if to ward off a blow, and moved slightly away from me.

"I don't know the man," she said.

"You deny that he called on you on Tuesday evening?"

"I do," she answered, in a steady voice.

I saw that she was rapidly recovering her self-control, and I made up my mind that I had misjudged the little woman. Under that soft, childish exterior must lie an indomitable will.

"Do you deny that you received a man on that evening?" She glanced hastily at each of us before answering: "No."

"Oh, you did see a gentleman? Who was he?"

She hesitated a moment: "An old friend."

"Will you kindly tell us his name?"

"No! I won't have him mixed up in this."

"Madam," said the detective, "the deceased has been murdered, and—" A shriek interrupted him.

"Murdered! Oh, no, no," she gasped, her eyes wide with terror.

"I regret to say that there is no doubt of it."

"But when,—how?" she demanded, in a trembling voice.

"On Tuesday night."

She drew a deep breath. The horror faded slowly from her face, and she repeated with great composure, "Oh, Tuesday night," with a slight emphasis on the Tuesday.

The change in her was perfectly startling. She seemed calm,—almost indifferent.

"Have you discovered how he was murdered?" she inquired.

"Yes; he was stabbed through the heart by an instrument no larger than a knitting-needle."

"How strange," she exclaimed; "do you know who committed the crime?"

"Not yet," said the Coroner; "and now, Mrs. Atkins, I ask you again if you are quite sure that you have never seen the deceased before?"

"Yes," she answered, firmly.

"And you are willing to testify to this effect?"

"Yes."

"You are aware that the elevator boy has positively identified the body as that of your visitor?"

"I guess my word's as good as a nigger's," she said, with a defiant toss of her head.

"No doubt," replied the Coroner, politely; "but if you would tell us the name and address of your friend we could look him up and be able to assure the police of his safety, and so save you the disagreeable necessity of appearing in court."

"In court," she repeated, with a horrified expression. Evidently this possibility had not occurred to her, and she glanced hurriedly around as if contemplating immediate flight.

"Mrs. Atkins," said the detective, earnestly, "I do not think that you realise certain facts. A man has been murdered who has been identified, rightly or wrongly, with your visitor. Now, no one saw your friend leave the building, and it is our business to ascertain that he did so. Can you tell us what became of him?"

A hunted expression came into her eyes, but she answered in a steady voice: "My friend left me at a little after eleven; he was going to take the midnight train to Boston." She paused. "His name is Allan Brown—there, now!"

"Thank you, madam, and what is Mr. Brown's address in Boston?"

"I don't know."

"What was his address in New York?"

"I'm sure I don't know."

"Was he in any business?"

"I don't know," she answered, sullenly, with a glance at the door.

"Mrs. Atkins, you seem singularly ignorant about your friend,—your old friend."

"Well, I hadn't seen him for some years. He's a stranger in the city."

"Where is his home?"

"I don't know," she answered, impatiently.

"Are you a New Yorker, Mrs. Atkins?" inquired the detective.

"No."

"Ah, I thought not! And where do you come from?"

"Chicago."

"Chicago? Indeed! I've been there some myself," Mr. Merritt continued, in a conversational tone. "Nice place. How long is it since you left there?"

"Six months," she answered, curtly.

"So it was in Chicago you knew your friend?"

"Yes," she admitted, with a slight start.

"And you are sure he didn't belong there?"

"Yes; but look here: why are you asking such a lot of questions about him? I've told you his name and where he's gone to, and if you can't find him that's your lookout."

"The consequences of our not being able to find him would be much more serious for you than for me," remarked Mr. Merritt, quietly.

"Now, Mrs. Atkins," resumed the Coroner, "can you say in what particular Mr. Brown differs from this dead man?"

"Oh, they're a good deal alike," she replied, fluently,—but I noticed that she did not look in the direction of the corpse,—"only Mr. Brown's younger, and not so heavy, and his nose is different. Still, the man does resemble Mr. Brown surprisingly. It gave me quite a shock when I first saw him." It certainly had, only I wondered if that were the true explanation.

"Please tell us what you did yesterday."

"I went out in the morning and I came home at about half-past five."

"What were you doing during all that time?"

"Oh, several things; I called on some friends and did some errands."

"Your husband has been out of town, I hear?"

"Yes."

"When did he leave the city?"

"On Tuesday morning."

"When did he return?"

"Last night."

"At what time?"

"Half-past one."

"Where did he come from?"

"Boston."

"But surely the Boston train gets in a good deal earlier than that!" the Coroner exclaimed.

"Yes, there had been a delay owing to a slight accident on the line," she reluctantly explained.

"Is Mr. Atkins often away?"

"Yes; he's out of town every week or so, on business."

"Thank you, Mrs. Atkins, that is all," the Coroner concluded, politely. But the lady was not so easily appeased, and flounced out of the room without deigning to glance at any of us.

The detective slipped out after her—to call the maids, as he explained, but it was five or six minutes before he returned with the waitress.

After answering several unimportant questions, the girl was asked whether she had ever seen the deceased before. "No, sir," she replied, promptly.

"Did anyone call on your mistress on Tuesday evening?"

"I can't say, sir; I was out."

"At what time did you go out?"

"At about a quarter to eight, sir."

"Where did you go to?"

"We went to a party at me sister's."

"Who do you mean by 'we'?"

"The cook and me, sir."

"Ah, the cook went out, too?"

"Yes, sir."

"Do you usually go out together?"

"No, sir."

"How did it happen that you did so on Tuesday?"

"Mr. Atkins, he was away, so Mrs. Atkins she said we might both go out."

"Mr. Atkins is often away from home, isn't he?"

"Yes, sir."

"How often?"

"About once a fortnight, sir."

"Has Mrs. Atkins ever allowed you both to go out together before?"

"No, sir."

"Where does your sister live, and what is her name?"

"Mrs. Moriarty, 300 Third Avenue."

The Coroner paused to scribble down the address, then resumed:

"At what time did you get back from the party?"

The girl tugged at her dress in some embarrassment. "It might have been after eleven," she reluctantly admitted.

"How much after—quarter past, half-past?" he suggested, as she still hesitated.

"It was almost half-past, sir."

"And when you returned, did you see your mistress?"

"Oh, yes, sir."

"Was she alone?"

"Yes, sir," the girl answered, with some surprise.

"Did you notice anything unusual about her?"

"Well, sir, she'd been crying, and I never see her cry before."

"What did Mrs. Atkins say to you?"

"She scolded us for being so late," the girl answered shamefacedly.

"Was that all she said?"

"Yes, sir."

"Where was your mistress when you saw her?"

"She was lying on the sofy in her bed-room, tired like."

"What did Mrs. Atkins do yesterday?"

"She went out after breakfast and didn't come back till nearly six."

"How did she seem when she returned?"

"She'd been crying awful, and she just lay quiet and wouldn't eat no dinner."

"Do Mr. and Mrs. Atkins get along well together?"

"Oh, sir, they're that loving," she answered with a blush and a smile.

Again my curiosity got the better of my discretion, and I asked: "Did you hear any strange noises during the night?"

The Coroner glared at me, but said nothing this time.

"Well," replied the girl, "me and Jane did think as we'd heard a scream."

Ha, ha, thought I, and I saw Mr. Merritt indulge in one of his quiet smiles.

"So you heard a scream," said the Coroner.

"I don't know for sure; I thought so."

"At what time did you hear it?"

"I don't know, sir; some time in thenight."

"What did you do when you heard it?"

"Nothing, sir."

This was all that could be got out of her, so she made way for the cook, who, after being cross-questioned at some length, did no more than corroborate the waitress's statement, only she was more positive of having heard the "screech" as she called it.

"Could you tell whether it was a man or woman who screamed?" inquired the Coroner.

"It was a woman's voice, sir."

Mr. Stuart, who was next admitted, proved to be a small, middle-aged man, extremely well groomed, and whom I recognized as one of the members of my Club, whose name I had never known. On being asked if he had ever seen the dead man before, he solemnly inserted a single eye-glass into his right eye, and contemplated the corpse with the greatest imperturbability.

"So far as I can remember, I have never seen the man before," he answered at last. After replying satisfactorily to a few more questions, he was allowed to retire, and his cook took his place. She was a large, stout woman about thirty years old, with a good deal of that coarse Southern beauty, which consists chiefly in snapping black eyes, masses of dark hair, and good teeth. On catching sight of the corpse, she threw up her hands and uttered a succession of squeals, which she seemed to consider due to the horror of the occasion, and then turned serenely towards the Coroner, and with a slight courtesy stood smilingly awaiting his questions.

"What is your name?" he inquired.

"Jeanne Alexandrine Argot," she replied.

"You are in the employ of Mr. Stuart?"

"Yes, sar. I 'ave been with Mr. Stuah, six a years, and he tell you——"

"Please look at the deceased, and tell me if you have ever seen him before?" the Coroner hastily interrupted.

"No, sar."

After answering a few more questions with overpowering volubility, she withdrew, and her husband entered. He was a tall, vigorous man, with large hawk-like eyes, apparently a good deal older than his wife. He bowed to us all on entering, and stood respectfully near the door, waiting to be spoken to.

"What is your name?" inquired the Coroner.

"Celestin Marie Argot."

"You work for Mr. Stuart?"

"Yes, sar; I am Meester Stuah's butlair."

"Look at this corpse, and tell me if you can identify it as that of any one you know, or have ever seen?"

He now glanced for the first time at the body, and I thought I saw his face contract slightly. But the expression was so fleeting that I could not be sure of it, and when he raised his head a few moments later he seemed perfectly composed and answered calmly: "I do not know ze man."

Apparently the Coroner was not completely satisfied, for he went on: "You know that this man has been murdered, and that it is your duty to give us any information that might lead to his identification. Have you seen any suspicious persons about the building during the last few days?"

"No, sar; nobody,"—but I thought he had hesitated an instant before answering.

"You must see a good many people pass up and down the back stairs," the detective remarked; "especially in this hot weather, when you must be obliged to leave the kitchen door open a good deal so as to get a draught."

The man cast a hurried, and I thought an apprehensive, glance at Mr. Merritt, and replied quickly: "Yes, sar; ze door is open almos' all ze time, but I 'ave seen nobody."

"Nobody?" repeated the detective.

"Yes, sar," Argot asserted, still more emphatically. "No vone, excep' ze butchair, ze bakair, and ze ozer tradesmen, of course."

"How early are you likely to open the kitchen door? To leave it open, I mean?"

"Oh, not till eight o'clock, perhap—Madame Argot, she stay in déshabille till zen."

"What time do you go to bed?"

"At ten o'clock generally, but some time eleven o'clock—even midnight— it depens."

"What time did you go to bed on Tuesday?"

"At eleven, sar."

"What had you been doing during the evening?"

"I had been at a restaurant wiz some friends."

"And when did you return?"

"At about half-pas' ten."

"Did you come in the back way?"

"Yes, sar."

"How did you get in?"

"My wife, she open ze door."

"And you saw nobody as you came in?"

He paused almost imperceptibly. "No, sar," he answered. But I was now convinced that he was holding something back.

"Very well; you can go," said the Coroner. The fellow bowed himself out with a good deal of quiet dignity.

"I kinder fancy that man knows something he won't tell," said the Coroner. "Now, we've seen every one but the workmen," he continued, wearily, mopping his forehead. "I don't believe one of them knows a thing; still, I've got to go through with it, I suppose," and going to the door he beckoned them all in.

There were five of them, including the foreman, and they appeared to be quiet, respectable young men. After looking at the dead man intently for some minutes, they all asserted that they had never laid eyes on him before.

"Now have any of you noticed during the three days you have been working here anybody who might have taken the key, kept it for some hours, and returned it without your noticing it?" inquired the Coroner.

"We've seen no strangers," the foreman replied, cautiously.

"Who have you seen?" The foreman was evidently prepared for this question.

"Well, sir, we've seen altogether six people: Jim, and Joe, and Tony, Mr. McGorry, Miss Derwent, and the Frinchman," he replied, checking them off on his fingers.

"When did the Frenchman come up here?"

"Yistidy morning, sir; he said he come to see the decorations, and he come again about three; but he didn't stay long. I warn't a-going to have him hanging round here interfering!"

"Did any of his actions at the time strike you as suspicious?"

"No, sir," acknowledged the foreman.

"And Miss Derwent; when did you see her?"

"I didn't see her myself in the morning, but he"—with a nod towards one of the men,—"he saw her look in as she was waiting for the elevator, and in the afternoon she come right in."

"Did she say anything?"

"Yes, sir; she said the paint and papers were mighty pretty."

"When you saw Miss Derwent," said the Coroner, addressing the man whom the foreman had pointed out, "what was she doing?"

"She was standing just inside the hall."

"Was her hand on the door knob?"

"I didn't notice, sir."

"Did the young lady say anything?"

"When she saw me a-looking at her, she just said: 'How pretty!' and went away."

"Have any of you seen Mr. or Mrs. Atkins, or either of their girls, since you have been working here?" They all replied in the negative.

The Coroner's physician turned up at this juncture, with many apologies for his late arrival, so, having no further excuse for remaining, I took my leave. The lower hall swarmed with innumerable reporters, trying to force their way upstairs, and who were only prevented from doing so by the infuriated McGorry and two or three stalwart policemen. On catching sight of me they all fell upon me with one accord, and I only managed to escape by giving them the most detailed description of the corpse and professing complete ignorance as to everything else.

CHAPTER VI

A LETTER AND ITS ANSWER

WHEN I got back to my diggings I was astonished to find that it was only ten o'clock. How little time it takes to change the whole world for one! All day long I forced myself to go about my usual work, but the thought of May Derwent never left me.

It was the greatest relief to find that in none of the evening papers did her name appear. How McGorry managed to conceal from the reporters the fact that she had been in the building remains a mystery to this day—but how thankful I was that he was able to do so! Already my greatest preoccupation was to preserve her fair name from the least breath of scandal. Not for an instant did I believe her to be connected with the murder;—on the other hand, I felt equally sure that she was in some great trouble, the nature of which I could not even guess. I longed to protect and help her, but how was I to do so, ignorant as I was of everything concerning her. I didn't even know where she was at that moment. At her mother's, perhaps. But where was that? Suddenly I remembered that my great friend, Fred Cowper, had mentioned in one of his recent letters that Mrs. Derwent and his mother were near neighbours in the country. To think that that lucky dog had been spending the last month within a stone's throw, perhaps, of her house—had seen her every day probably, and had been allowed these inestimable privileges simply because he had broken an old leg! And I, who would gladly have sacrificed both legs to have been in his place, was forced to remain in New York because—forsooth!—of an apoplectic old patient—who refused either to live or die! Well, as I couldn't go to her, it was at any rate a comfort to be able to get news of her so easily— so seizing a pen, I hastily scratched off the following note:

NEW YORK,
August 10, 1898.

DEAR FRED:

You know me pretty well and know therefore that I'm not a prying sort of fellow—don't you? So that when I ask you to tell me all you know about Miss May Derwent—I hope you will believe that I am animated by no idle curiosity. A doctor is often forced to carry more secrets than a family solicitor, and is as much in honor bound. Through no fault of my own, I have come into the possession of certain facts relating to Miss Derwent which lead me to believe that she is in great trouble. Furthermore, I am convinced that I could help her, were I not handicapped by my very slight personal acquaintance with her, but more than that by my entire ignorance regarding certain details of her life. I might as well acknowledge that I am interested in the young lady, and am anxious to serve her if I can. But if I am to do so, I must first find out a few particulars of her life, and these I hope you can give me.

In the first place I want to know whether she has any young male relative who is tall, with good figure? I remember hearing that she is an only child, but has she no cousin with whom she is on terms of brotherly intimacy?

Secondly, Is she engaged, or reported to be engaged, and if so, to whom?

Thirdly, What are the names of her most favored suitors?

Fourthly, What lady does she know intimately who has very dark hair, and is also slight and tall?

I don't need to tell you to treat this letter as absolutely confidential, nor to assure you again that only the deepest interest in Miss Derwent, and the conviction that she is in need of help, induce me to pry into her affairs.

More than this I cannot tell you, so don't ask me.

Good-night, old chap! Hope your leg is getting on all right.

Affectionately yours,
CHARLES K. FORTESCUE.

HOPE FARM, BEVERLEY, L. I.,
Friday, August 11.

DEAR CHARLEY,—You may imagine how exciting I found your letter when I tell you that I have known May Derwent since she was a tiny tot, and that their country place is not half a mile from here. She is exactly my sister Alice's age, and I have never known her very well till she came out last winter, for eight years make a big barrier between children. I like and admire May extremely, for not only is she a very beautiful girl, but an extremely nice one, as well. Difficult as it may be to explain certain things, I am sure that, whatever the trouble she is in, if you knew the whole truth, you would find it only redounded to her credit. She is an impulsive, warm-hearted and rather tempestuous child—generous, loyal, and truthful to a fault. I have just been discreetly sounding Alice about her, and asked why I had not seen May since I had been down here this time, as on former occasions she used always to be running in and out of the house. And Alice tells me that for the last three months May has been a changed being. From a happy, thoughtless girl, overflowing with health and spirits, she has become a listless, self-contained, almost morose woman. She refuses to go anywhere, and spends most of her time either in her own room or taking long solitary walks or rides. The doctor talks of nervous prostration, but do you think it likely that a vigorous, athletic young girl would develop nerves solely in consequence of a few months' gaiety during the winter? It seems to me incredible, and so I am forced to believe that May has something on her mind which is reacting on her body, causing her to shun all the things she used to delight in. Now, when a young, rich, beautiful, and sought-after girl suddenly takes to avoiding her species, and becomes pale and melancholy, the usual explanation is—an unhappy love affair. And, of course, that may still turn out to be the truth in this case; but in the meantime I have another hypothesis to suggest, that seems to me to fit in with the known facts even better than the other.

May Derwent is not an only child, but has, or at any rate had, a brother about ten years older than herself who, I confess, was one of the heroes of my childhood. Only a little older than the rest of us boys, he was much bigger and stronger. He was the leader of all our games, and the instigator of our most outrageous exploits. He was the horror of all parents and the delight of all children. Cruel, vindictive, untruthful, leaving others to pay the penalty for his faults whenever it was possible, he was not a nice boy even in those early days, but then he was so handsome, so bold and unscrupulous, so inspired in devising new crimes for us to commit, that it is hardly to be wondered at that he was at the same time our terror and our idol. His school record was bad; his college record was worse, till one fine day he suddenly and mysteriously disappeared from Harvard, and has never been heard of since. What had occurred I never could find out; that it was something very disgraceful I am sure, for his mother, whose pride and hope he had been, never again mentioned his name.

Now, don't you think it quite possible that he may have returned and been bothering his sister in some way? She may be either trying to shield him from still greater disgrace, or be endeavouring to spare her mother the further knowledge of his misdeeds. Mind you, these are all merely the wildest conjectures.

As for May's lovers, their name is simply legion, including young Norman, the millionaire, Sir Arthur Trevor, Guy Weatherby and a painter chap—Greywood, I think his name is. Mère Derwent, I believe, favors Norman's suit, having (sensible woman!) a great faith in American husbands, but there is a rumour that May, with the perversity of her sex, is inclined to smile on the young artist, who, I am told is an affected chap, just back from Paris, without either money or talent. But no doubt he strikes her as a more romantic lover than good old Norman, who is the best of fellows, and absolutely eligible in every way.

Alice tells me that May has appeared quite eager for her Bar Harbor visit, notwithstanding that she has refused all other invitations, and Mrs. Derwent has had great hopes that the change would do her good.

What you have told me is no small tax on my discretion, but what you have refrained from telling taxes my curiosity far more. But notice—I ask no questions!!

By the way, why don't you come down and spend next Sunday with us? You might see the lovely May again,—who knows?

Affectionately yours,

FRED.

CHAPTER VII

MR. MERRITT INSTRUCTS ME

F RED'S letter was a great relief to me. I had not dared to allow my thoughts to dwell on the man whom I had seen in May Derwent's apartment on that eventful night. The supposition, however, that it was her brother, explained everything satisfactorily. Nothing could be more likely than that this angel of mercy should give shelter to this returned prodigal, and try to save him from the punishment he so richly deserved. But what cared I what *he* had done? She—she—was immaculate.

At the hospital that morning, I was in such good spirits that I had some difficulty in keeping my elation within bounds. As it was, I noticed that several nurses eyed me with suspicion.

My preoccupation about Miss Derwent's affairs had been so great that I had hardly given a thought to the mysterious murder, and was consequently very much surprised, on returning home that afternoon, to find the detective patiently awaiting me.

"Well, Mr. Merritt," I exclaimed; "glad to see you; what can I do for you? Anything wrong with your heart, or your liver, or your nerves, eh?"

"Well, Doctor, I guess my nerves are pretty near all right," he answered, with a slow smile.

"I'm glad to hear it. Won't you sit down?"

He selected a comfortable chair, and we sat down facing each other. I wondered what could be coming next.

"Now, Doctor," he began, in a matter-of-fact voice, "I'd like you to tell me all you know of the murder."

He had taken me completely by surprise, but I am learning to control my features, and flatter myself that I did not move a muscle as I quietly replied:

"This is a very strange question, and I can only answer that I know nothing."

"Oh, hardly as little as that," the detective rejoined, with irritating complacency.

"Just as little as that," I asserted, with some warmth.

"Well, Doctor, if that is the case, you can no doubt explain a few things that have been puzzling me. In the first place, will you tell me why, if you were not expecting another victim, you showed such surprise at the sight of the corpse? What reason could you have had for being so deeply interested in the relative positions of your roof—not your office, mind you, but your roof— and the room in which the body was found, unless you had noticed something unusual from that point of observation? Why were you so sure that the Derwent's flat was occupied, if you had not seen some person or persons there? By the way, I noticed that from your roof I could look directly into their windows. Again, you betrayed great surprise when Miss Derwent lifted her veil. Why did you do so, except that you had previously seen a very different looking person in her apartment? And why did you select the Atkins's two servants out of all the people in the building, to question about a certain noise, but that you yourself had heard a scream coming from their premises? And, lastly, you showed an unexplained interest in the back door of the Rosemere, which is particularly suggestive in view of the fact that this window is exactly opposite to it. I need only add that your presence on the roof during some part of Wednesday night, or early Thursday morning, is attested by the fact that I found some pipe-ash near the chimney. You smoke a pipe, I see" (pointing to a rack full of them); "your janitor does not, neither do your two fellow-lodgers. Besides that, all the other occupants of this house are willing to swear that they have not been on the roof recently, and those ashes could not have been long where I found them; the wind would have scattered them. You see, I know very little, but I know enough to be sure that you know more."

I was perfectly dumbfounded, and gazed at the detective for some moments without speaking.

"Well, granted that I was on the roof during a part of Wednesday night, what of it? And if I did hear or see anything suspicious, how can you prove it, and above all, how can you make me tell you of it?"

"I can't," rejoined Mr. Merritt, cheerfully. "I can only ask you to do so."

"And if I refuse?"

"Then I shall have to delay satisfying my curiosity till we meet in court, but I do not doubt that my patience will then be adequately rewarded, for a skilful lawyer will surely be able to get at many details that would escape me, and I hardly think that you would resort to perjury to shield two women whom I am convinced you never laid eyes on before yesterday, and have certainly not seen since." The detective paused.

I still hesitated, for I felt an extreme reluctance to further compromise that

44

poor girl by anything I might say.

"Come, Doctor," he urged, leaning forward and placing his hand on my knee, "don't you think it would be better for all parties for you to tell me what you know? I am as anxious to shield the innocent as you can be. By withholding valuable information you may force me to put a young lady through a very trying and public ordeal, which I am sure might be easily spared her, if I only knew a few more facts of the case."

This last argument decided me, and making a virtue of necessity I gave him a minute account of all I had seen and heard. When I came to describing the man's prolonged search Mr. Merritt nodded several times with great satisfaction.

"Can't you tell me a little more how this man looked?" he eagerly inquired. "You must have seen him pretty clearly while he was moving around that lighted room. Had he any hair on his face?"

"Well," I confessed, "it is a funny thing, but I can't for the life of me remember; I've tried to; sometimes I think he was clean shaven, and again I am sure he had a small moustache."

The detective glared at me for a moment; it was difficult for him to forgive such aggravating lack of memory. To be given such an opportunity and to foozel it! He heaved a sigh of resignation as he inquired:

"Can you remember how he was dressed?"

"Oh, yes," I replied with alacrity, anxious to retrieve myself, "he had on a white shirt and dark trousers, and his sleeves were rolled back."

"Did he close the windows before he left?"

"Yes, and he pulled down the blinds also."

"You are sure that you saw no one in the apartment resembling Miss Derwent?"

"Quite sure; the woman I saw was taller and had flat, black hair."

"What do you mean by 'flat'?"

"Why, nowadays girls wear their hair loose; it bulges away from their faces; but hers lay tight to her head in a flat, black mass," I explained.

I then harped on the probability of the return of Miss May's prodigal brother, and suggested the possibility that the dark-haired woman might be his wife.

"Well, well, Doctor! This is all very interesting. The story of the brother, especially. You see, I had already discovered that a man had spent many hours in her apartment——"

"How did you find that out?" I interrupted.

"Oh, quite easily," rejoined the detective; "as soon as all the excitement was over yesterday, I made McGorry open the Derwent's apartments for me. You may imagine what a fuss he made about it. Well anyhow he got me——"

"But why did you want to get in?" I inquired; "did you suspect her?"

"No," he replied, "I did not. But in my profession you take no chances. Impressions, intuitions, are often of great value, only you must be careful always to verify them. I was almost sure that the young lady was innocent, but it was my business to prove her so. Now, it is certain that the person, or persons, who smuggled the corpse into the room where it was found, must, at one time or another, have had the key of that apartment in their possession, and there are only three people whom we know of as yet who were in a position to have had it. These three are: Miss Derwent, the French butler, and, of course, McGorry. So far I have not been able to connect the latter two, even in the most indirect way, with the catastrophe. Unfortunately, that is not the case with the young lady. One person, at least, has identified the body as that of her visitor, and your behaviour," he added, with a smile, "led me to believe that you suspected her of something. Not of the crime, I felt sure of that, but of *what*, then? I determined to find out, and now that I have done so, let me tell you that I am still convinced of her innocence."

I jumped up and shook him by the hand. "So am I, so am I," I exclaimed.

"But this is a very queer case," he continued, "and I shall need all the assistance you can give me, if——"

"You shall have it," I broke in, enthusiastically; "anything I can do. But tell me, first, how you found out about Miss Derwent's brother?"

"Not so fast, young man! At present, we know nothing about a brother. I only said that I had discovered in the apartment traces of the recent and prolonged presence of a man, and I may add of a man of some means."

"How did you find that out? Especially about his means?" I inquired, with a smile.

"Quite easily. In the parlor, which was the first room I entered, I noticed that every piece of furniture had been lately moved from its place. Now, this was too heavy a job for a girl to have undertaken single-handed. Who helped her, I wondered? Her visitor of Tuesday evening might have been the person, but for various reasons I was inclined to doubt it. I thought it more likely to have been the woman whose existence your behaviour had led me to infer. I next examined the dining-room. A few crumbs showed that it had been used, but I could find no traces of her mysterious companion. The library had not even been entered. On the floor above, the front bedroom alone showed signs of recent occupation. Two crumpled sheets were still on the bed, and in the drawers were several articles of woman's apparel. Returning to the lower floor by the back stairs, I found myself in the kitchen. Here, in the most unexpected place, I discovered an important clue." Mr. Merritt paused, and looked at me with a gleam of triumph in his eye.

"Yes, yes, and what was that?" I inquired, breathlessly.

"Only the odor, the very faintest ghost of an odor, I may say, of cigar-smoke."

"In the kitchen?" I exclaimed, incredulously.

"In the kitchen," repeated the detective. "I at once drew up the blinds, and looked out. The window opened directly on the fire escape, with nothing opposite but the roofs of some low houses. Pulling out my magnifying glass, I crawled out. I soon satisfied myself that the stairs leading up and down had not been recently used; on the other hand, I was equally sure that someone had very lately been out on the small landing. So I sat down there and looked about me. I could see nothing. At last, by peering through the bars of the iron flooring, I thought I could discern a small brown object, caught in between the slats of the landing below. I climbed down there mighty quick, I can tell you, and in a moment held the butt end of a cigar in my hand. It was, as I had suspected, from the delicate odor it had left behind, one which had cost about fifty cents. I now extended my search downward, and examined every window-sill, every crevice, till I reached the basement, and, as a result of my hunt, I collected five cigar stumps, all of the same brand. From the number, I concluded that whoever had been in the apartment had been there a considerable time. From his only smoking in the kitchen or on the fire-escape, I gathered that he was anxious to leave no traces of his presence; and lastly, from the quality of his cigars, I judged him to be a man of means. So you see I had discovered, even without your assistance, that, although Miss Derwent may have told us the truth, she certainly had not told us all of it."

I nodded gloomily.

"What you tell me of this dark-haired woman is still more puzzling," the detective continued. "She has covered up her tracks so well that not only did I find no trace of her, but no one, not even yourself, saw her either enter or leave the building. And I should never have dreamed of her existence if I had not noticed your surprise when Miss Derwent lifted her veil. Now, the first thing to be done is to try and find this strange couple, and we will begin by tracing the man whom you saw leaving the Rosemere with a market-basket. It will be easy enough to find out if he is nothing but a local tradesman, and if he is *not*, then in all probability he is the man we want. The detective who is watching Miss Derwent——"

"A detective watching Miss Derwent!" I exclaimed.

"Why, yes. What did you expect? I sent one down with her to the country yesterday."

Perhaps I ought to have been prepared for it, but the idea of a common fellow dogging May Derwent's footsteps, was quite a shock to me, so I inquired, with considerable ill-humor: "And what does he report?"

"Nothing much. The young lady returned to her mother, as she said she would, and since then has kept to her room, but has refused to see a doctor."

"Have you discovered yet who the dead man really is?" I asked, after a slight pause.

"No," answered the detective, with a troubled look, "and I can't make it out. Jim and Joe each persists in his own identification. I expected Jim to weaken, he seemed so much less positive at first, but whether he has talked himself into the belief that the corpse is that of the young lady's visitor, or whether it really does resemble him so much as to give the boy grounds for thinking so, I can't make out."

"I see, however, that *you* believe the murdered man to be Mrs. Atkins's friend, of whose history and whereabouts she was so strangely ignorant."

"Well, I don't know," the detective replied. "We have found out that an Allan Brown did engage a berth on the midnight train to Boston."

"Really? Why, I was sure that Allan Brown was a creation of the little lady's imagination. By the way, it is a strange coincidence that two mysterious Allans are connected with this case."

"Yes, I have thought of that," the detective murmured; "and Allan is no common name, either. But it is a still stranger circumstance that neither of Allan Brown nor of the murdered man (I am now taking for granted that they are not identical) can we discover the slightest trace beyond the solitary fact that an upper berth on the Boston train was bought on Tuesday afternoon, by a person giving the former's name, and whose description applies, of course, equally to both. Mrs. Atkins volunteers the information that Brown was a stranger in the city, and so far I have no reason to doubt it. Now, a man who can afford to wear a dress suit, and who is a friend of a woman like Mrs.

Atkins, presumably had fairly decent quarters while he was in town. And yet inquiries have been made at every hotel and boarding-house, from the cheapest to the most expensive, and not one of them knows anything of an Allan Brown, nor do they recognize his description as applying to any of their late guests. The deceased, of course, may have had rooms somewhere, or a flat, or even a house, in which case it will take longer to trace him; although even so, it is remarkable that after such wide publicity has been given to his description, no one has come forward and reported him as missing. The morgue has been crowded with idle sightseers, but nobody as yet claims to have seen the victim before."

"That is queer," I assented, "especially as the dead man was in all probability a person of some prominence. He certainly must have been rich. The pearl studs he wore were very fine."

"Oh, those were imitation pearls," said the detective, "and I am inclined to think that, far from being wealthy, he was, at the time of his death, extremely badly off, although other indications point to his having seen better days."

"Really!" I exclaimed.

"Yes; didn't you notice that his clothes, although evidently expensive, were all decidedly shabby? That his silk socks were almost worn out; that his pumps were down at the heel?"

"Yes, I did notice something of the kind."

"But those large imitation pearls blinded you to everything else, I see," Mr. Merritt remarked, with a smile.

"I suppose so," I acknowledged; "they and the sleeve-links with the crest."

"Ah, those are really interesting, and for the first time in my life I find myself wishing that we were more careful in this country about the use of such things. Unfortunately, we are so promiscuous and casual in adopting any coat-of-arms that happens to strike our fancy that the links become almost valueless as a clue. Still, I have sent one of them to an authority in heraldry, and shall be much interested to hear what he has to say about it. By the way, did anything else strike you as peculiar about the corpse?"

"No," I answered, after a moment's reflection.

"It did not seem to you odd that no hat was found with the body?"

"Dear me! I never noticed that. How singular! What could have become of it?"

"Ah, if we only knew that we should be in a fair way to solving this mystery. For I have found out that, whereas the description of Miss Derwent's visitor and Mrs. Atkins's friend tally on all other points, they differ radically on this one. The former wore a panama, whereas the latter wore an ordinary straw hat. Now, one of those hats must be somewhere in the Rosemere, and yet I can't find it."

"Mr. Merritt," I inquired, "have you any theory as to the motive of this murder?"

"Not as yet," he replied. "It may have been jealousy, revenge, or a desire to be rid of a dangerous enemy, and if you had not given it as your opinion that the man met his death while wholly or semi-unconscious, I should have added self-defence to my list of possibilities. The only thing I am pretty sure of is— that the motive was not robbery."

"Look here, Mr. Merritt, I can't help wondering that, whereas you have treated Miss Derwent with the utmost suspicion, have made a thorough search of her apartment, and have even sent a sleuth to watch her, yet you have shown such indifference to Mrs. Atkins's movements. Surely suspicion points quite as strongly to her as to the young lady?"

"No, it doesn't," replied the detective. "The key! You forget the key cannot so far be connected with her. But, may I ask, who told you that I had neglected to make inquiries about the lady?"

"Nobody; I only inferred," I stammered.

"You were wrong," continued Mr. Merritt. "I have made every possible inquiry about Mrs. Atkins. I have even sent a man to Chicago to find out further particulars, although I have already collected a good deal of interesting information about the little lady's past life."

"Really? And was there anything peculiar about it?"

"No; I can't exactly say there was. Mrs. Atkins is the only daughter of a wealthy saloon-keeper, John Day by name, and is twenty-six years old. Nothing is known against her except that in that city she chose her companions from amongst a very fast crowd. There is also a rumor, which the Chicago detective has not been able to verify, that when she was about sixteen or seventeen years old, she eloped with an Eastern man, from whom she was almost immediately divorced. At any rate, she has been known for a good many years as Miss Day, and has lived at home with her father. The memory of her marriage, if indeed she ever was married, has grown so dim that a great many people, among whom may be numbered some of her intimate friends, have never heard of it, and vehemently deny the whole story. I hope, however, soon to find out the facts of the case. Young Atkins met his wife last winter at Atlantic City, and at once fell in love with her. His father, who is a very wealthy contractor, was strongly opposed to the match. He was very ambitious for his son, and thought the daughter of a saloon-keeper, whose reputation was none of the best, was no desirable wife for his boy."

"But they married in spite of him," I said.

"Yes, and old man Atkins has become reconciled to them, and makes them a very handsome allowance."

"How long have they been married?" I asked.

"Since the fifteenth of April," replied the detective, "and they were not married in Chicago, but in this city. I guess the lady was not over anxious to introduce her husband to her former pals."

"I suppose you have searched her apartment for a possible clue,—the hat, for instance?"

"Yes, but as she has not been out since Wednesday, I have not been able to make as thorough a search as I should like. She is a shy bird, and I don't want to frighten her till I have a few more facts to go on. If she thinks herself watched she may become wary, while now, I hope she will make use of her fancied security to do something which may give us a lead."

"Well, Mr. Merritt, I conclude from all this that, although you are unable to trace the possession of the key to Mrs. Atkins, nevertheless, your suspicions point towards her?"

"Certainly not. There is nothing to connect her with the tragedy, except the fact that one negro boy identified the corpse as that of one of her visitors. On the contrary, the more I look into this case, the less do I see how the lady could be involved in it. Let us suppose that she did kill the man. Where could she have secreted him during the twenty-four hours that must have elapsed before the body was finally disposed of? The only place of concealment on the lower floor of her apartment is a coat closet under the stairs, and I doubt very much whether a small, unmuscular woman like Mrs. Atkins is capable of dragging so large a man even for a short distance."

"But," I suggested, "the murder may have been committed in the hall, just a step from this hiding-place."

"Yes, that is, of course, possible. But there is still another objection. The closet is so small that I do not believe a man could be got into it without doubling him up, and of that the body shows no signs. Besides, if Mrs. Atkins is guilty, we must believe her husband to be her accomplice, for who else could have helped her hide her victim? Now, you must know that the Atkins men, both father and son, bear most excellent reputations, especially the young man, of whom every one speaks in the highest terms, and I do not think that a person unaccustomed to deceit could have behaved with such perfect composure in the presence of a corpse of which he had criminal knowledge."

"But he did show some emotion," I urged.

"Oh, yes; I know what you mean,—when he learned that the man was murdered on Tuesday night he seemed startled."

"Well, how do you account for that?"

"I don't account for it. Why, Doctor, in a case like this there are a hundred things I can't account for. For instance, what was the cause of Mrs. Atkins's scream? You have no idea; neither have I. Why did she show such emotion at the sight of the corpse? I am not prepared to say. Why did she appear so relieved when she heard that the murder occurred on Tuesday? I can formulate no plausible explanation for it. And these are only a few of the rocks that I am running up against all the time."

"But look here. If you really believe Miss Derwent and Mrs. Atkins both innocent, who do you think killed the man?"

"I don't know. Oh, I am aware that the detective of fiction is always supposed to be omniscient, but my profession, Doctor, is just like any other. There is no hocus-pocus about it. To succeed in it requires, in the first place, accurate and most minute powers of observation, unlimited patience, the capacity for putting two and two together. Add to this an unprejudiced mind, and last, but not least, respect, amounting to reverence, for any established *fact*. Now, the only *facts* we have as yet gathered about this murder are: that the man was young, dissipated, and was stabbed through the heart by some very small instrument or weapon; that his assailant was an inmate of the Rosemere; that the crime was committed on Tuesday night; and, lastly, that whoever placed the body where it was found must, at one time or another, have had the key to the outside door in his or her possession. Whatever else we may think or believe, is purely speculative. We presume, for instance, that the man was poor. As for the other facts we have gleaned about the different inmates of the building, till we know which one of them had a hand in this tragedy, we cannot consider what we have learned about them as throwing any light on the murder. About that, as I said before, we know mighty little, and even that little is the result of thirty-eight hours' work, not of one man alone, but of seven or eight."

"Indeed!" I exclaimed.

"Now, both ladies deny that they knew the deceased, and perhaps they are right. It is, of course, possible that there was a third man in the building that evening, who was also tall, dark, and wore a pointed beard. It is not likely, however. Such a coincidence is almost unheard of. Still it is possible, and that possibility must be reckoned with. Now, I must be off," said Mr. Merritt, rising abruptly from his chair, "and if you hear any more of the young lady's movements, let me know. There's my address. In the meantime, thank you very much for what you have already told me." And before I could get out one of the twenty questions that were still burning on my lips, the man was gone.

For some minutes I sat quite still, too miserable to think connectedly. Alas! my fears had not been groundless. The poor girl was in even greater trouble than I had supposed. I believed the detective to be a decent chap, who would keep his mouth shut, but how dreadful to think that her reputation depended on the discretion of any man. Should it become known that she had received one young man alone in an empty apartment, while another was seen there at three o'clock in the morning, it would mean social death to her. Oh, for the right to offer her my protection, my services!

Of course, it was now absolutely necessary to trace the man who spent Tuesday evening with her, and to prove beyond doubt that he was still alive. I wished that this might be done without her knowledge, so as to spare her the shock of finding herself suspected of a crime.

Again I thought of Fred, and at once sent him a few lines, begging him to let me know whether he or his sister knew of any friend or admirer of Miss Derwent who resembled the enclosed description, and if either of them did know of such a person, please to telegraph me the man's name, and, if possible, his address. While giving no reasons for my questions, I again enjoined the greatest secrecy.

CHAPTER VIII

AN IDENTIFICATION

TELEGRAM.

DR. CHARLES FORTESCUE,
  MADISON AVENUE,
    NEW YORK CITY.

SATURDAY, August 12.

Maurice Greywood. Can't find his address. May be in Directory.

FREDERIC COWPER.

Clipping from the New York *Bugle*, Sunday, August 13.

LANDLADY IDENTIFIES BODY OF THE ROSEMERE VICTIM AS THAT OF HER VANISHED LODGER, ARTIST GREYWOOD. POLICE STILL SCEPTICAL.

Mr. Maurice Greywood, the talented young artist who returned from Paris the beginning of last winter, has disappeared, and grave fears for his safety are entertained. He was last seen in his studio, 188 Washington Square, early on Tuesday, August 8th, by Mrs. Kate Mulroy, the janitress. Ever since the young artist moved into the building, Mrs. Mulroy has taken complete charge of his rooms, but, owing to a disagreement which took place between them last Tuesday, she has ceased these attentions. Yesterday evening, while looking over a copy of the *Bugle* of the preceding day, Mrs. Mulroy came across the portrait of the unknown man whose murdered body was discovered under very mysterious circumstances in an unoccupied apartment of the Rosemere, corner of —— Street and Madison Avenue, on the preceding Thursday. She at once recognized it as bearing a striking resemblance to her lodger. Thoroughly alarmed she decided to investigate the matter. After knocking several times at Mr. Greywood's door, without receiving an answer, she opened it by means of a pass-key. Both the studio and bedroom were in the greatest confusion, and from the amount of dust that had accumulated over everything, she concluded that the premises had not been entered for several days. Her worst fears being thus confirmed, she hastened at once to the Morgue, and requested to see the body of the Rosemere victim, which she immediately identified as that of Maurice Greywood.

Strangely enough, the police throw doubts on this identification, although they acknowledge that they have no other clue to go on. However, Mrs. Greywood, the young man's mother, has been sent for, and is expected to arrive to-morrow from Maine, where she is spending the summer.

The people at the Rosemere are still foolishly trying to make a mystery of the murder, and refuse all information [etc., etc.].

TO DR. CHARLES K. FORTESCUE FROM DR. FREDERIC COWPER, BEVERLEY, L. I.

SUNDAY EVENING, August 13th.

DEAR CHARLEY:

No sooner had I read in to-day's paper that the body found in the Rosemere had been identified as that of Maurice Greywood, than I knew at once why you have taken such an interest in poor May. I see now that you have suspected from the first that the murdered man was not unknown to her, and your last letter, describing her "friend," proves to me beyond doubt that you were ignorant of nothing but his name, for Greywood and no other answers exactly to that description. How you found out what you did, I can't imagine; but remembering that your office window commands a view of the entrance to the building, I think it possible that you may have seen something from that point of vantage, which enabled you to put two and two together. But I wonder that I can feel any surprise at your having discovered the truth, when the truth itself is unbelievable!! May Derwent is incapable of killing any one —no matter what provocation she may have had. She is incapable of a dishonourable action, and above all things incapable of an intrigue. She is purity itself. I swear it. And yet what are the facts that confront us? A man, known to have been her professed suitor, is found dead in a room adjoining her apartment, dead with a wound through his heart—a wound, too, caused by a knitting-needle or hat-pin, as you yourself testified! And before trying to find out who killed him we must first think of some reasonable excuse for his having been at the Rosemere at all. How strange that he should happen to go to the building at the very time when May (who was supposed to be on her way to Bar Harbor, mind you!) was there also. Who was he calling on, if not on her?

Luckily, no one as yet seems to have thought of her in connection with Greywood's death. My sister has, in fact, been wondering all day whom he could have been visiting when he met his tragic fate. But, sooner or later, the truth will become known, and then—? Even in imagination I can't face that possibility.

And now, since you have discovered so much, and as I believe you to be as anxious as I am to help this poor girl, I am going to accede to your request and tell you all that I have been able to find out about the sad affair. I know that I run the risk of being misunderstood—even by you—and accused of unpardonable indiscretion. But it seems to me that in a case like this no ordinary rules hold good, and that in order to preserve a secret, one has sometimes to violate a confidence.

I have discovered—but I had better begin at the beginning, and tell you as accurately and circumstantially as possible how the following facts became known to me, so that you may be better able to judge of their value. Truth, after all, is no marble goddess, unchangeable, immovable, but a very chameleon taking the colour of her surroundings. A detached sentence, for instance, may mean a hundred things according to the when, where, and how of its utterance. But enough of apologies—*Qui s'excuse, s'accuse.*

So here goes.

I spent the morning on our piazza, and as I lay there, listening to the faint strains of familiar hymns which floated to me through the open windows of our village church, I could not help thinking that those peaceful sounds made a strange accompaniment to my gloomy and distracted thoughts. I longed to see May and judge for myself how things stood with her. I was therefore especially glad after the service was over to see Mrs. Derwent turn in at our gate. She often drops in on her way from church to chat a few minutes with my mother. But I soon became convinced that the real object of her visit to-day was to see me. Why, I could not guess. The dear lady, usually so calm and dignified, positively fidgeted, and several times forgot what she was saying, and remained for a minute or so with her large eyes fastened silently upon me, till, noticing my embarrassment, she recovered herself with a start and plunged into a new topic of conversation. At last my mother, feeling herself *de trop*, made some excuse, and went into the house. But even then Mrs. Derwent did not immediately speak, but sat nervously clasping and unclasping her long, narrow hands.

"Fred," she said at last, "I have known you ever since you were a little boy, and as I am in great trouble I have come to you, hoping that you will be able to help me."

"Dear Mrs. Derwent, you know there is nothing I would not do for you and yours," I replied.

"It is May that I want to speak to you about; she is really very ill, I fear."

"Indeed, I am sorry to hear it; what is the matter with her?"

"I don't know. She has not been herself for some time."

"So I hear. Do you know of any reason for her ill health?"

"She has not been exactly ill," she explained, "only out of sorts. Yes, I'm afraid I do know why she has changed so lately."

"Really," I exclaimed, much interested.

"Yes, it has all been so unfortunate," she continued. "You know how much admiration May received last winter; she had several excellent offers, any one of which I should have been perfectly willing to have her accept. Naturally, I am not anxious to have her marry, at least not yet; for when my child leaves me, what is there left for me in life? Still, one cannot think of that, and if she had chosen a possible person I should gladly have given my consent. But the only one she seemed to fancy was a most objectionable young man, an artist; *the* Maurice Greywood, in fact, of whose supposed murder you no doubt read in this morning's paper."

"Yes," I admitted.

"Well, I put my foot down on that. I told her she would break my heart if she persisted in marrying the fellow. It was really a shock to me to find that a daughter of mine had so little discrimination as even to like such a person; but she is young and romantic, and the creature is handsome, and clever in a Brummagem way. The man is a fakir, a *poseur*! I even suspect, Fred, that his admiration for May is not quite disinterested, and that he has a very keen eye to her supposed bank account."

"But May is such a lovely girl——"

"Oh, yes. I know all about that," interrupted Mrs. Derwent, "but in this case '*les beaux yeux de la cassette*' count for something, I am sure. He has absolutely no means of his own, and a profession which may keep him in gloves and cigarettes. I hear that he is supported by his mother and friends. Think of it! No, no, I could not bear her to marry that sort of man. But the child, for she is little more, took my refusal much to heart, fancied herself a martyr no doubt, and grew so pale and thin that I consulted the doctor here about her. He suggested nervous prostration, due to too much excitement, and wanted her to take a rest cure. I am sure, however, that that is all nonsense. May was simply fretting herself sick; she *wanted* to be ill, I think, so as to punish me for my obduracy."

"But what, then, makes you so anxious about her now?" I inquired. "Have any new symptoms developed?"

"Yes," and after glancing anxiously about to see whether she could be overheard, Mrs. Derwent continued in a lower voice. "You know that she started to go to Bar Harbor last Tuesday." I nodded. "Well, she seemed really looking forward to her visit, and when she left home was very affectionate to me, and more like her old self than she had been for months. But through some carelessness she missed her connection in town, and instead of returning here as she ought to have done, spent two nights in our empty apartment—of all places!! What possessed her to do such a thing I cannot find out, and she is at present so extremely excitable that I do not dare to insist on an explanation. When she did return here on Thursday she told me at once about the murder and how she was made to look at the body and to give an account of herself. Of course, we were very much afraid that her name would get into the papers and all the facts of her escapade become known. Through some miracle, that at least has been spared me; but the shock of being brought into such close contact with a mysterious crime has proved too much for the child's nerves, and she is in such an overwrought hysterical condition that I am seriously alarmed about her. I wanted to send again for Dr. Bertrand. He is not very brilliant, but I thought he might at least give her a soothing draught. She wept bitterly, however, at the bare idea—insisted that he only made her more nervous. I then suggested sending for our New York physician, but she became quite violent. Really I could hardly recognise May, she was so——so—impossible. Of course she is ill, and I now fear seriously so."

Mrs. Derwent paused to wipe her eyes.

"When you say that she is violent and impossible, what do you mean, exactly?"

"It is difficult to give you an idea of how she has been behaving, Fred, but here is an instance that may show how extraordinary her conduct has been: Her room is next to mine, and since her return from town she has shut herself up there quite early every evening. I know she doesn't sleep much, for I hear her moving about all night long. When I have gone to her door, however, and asked her what was the matter, she has answered me quite curtly, and refused to let me in. She has not been out of the house since she came back, but, strangely enough, I have caught her again and again peering through the blinds of those rooms that have a view of the road, just as if she were watching for somebody. As soon as she sees that she is observed, she frowns and moves away. Last night I slept very heavily, being completely worn out by all this anxiety, and was suddenly awakened by a piercing shriek. I rushed into May's room and found her sitting up in bed talking volubly, while about her all the lights were blazing. 'Take him away, take him away!' she kept repeating, and then she wailed: 'Oh, he's dead, he's dead!' I saw at once that she was asleep and tried to rouse her, but it was some time before I succeeded in doing so. I told her she had been dreaming, but she showed no curiosity as to what she might have been saying, only evincing a strong desire to be left alone. As I was leaving the room, I noticed that the key-hole had been carefully stopped up. I suppose she did that so as to prevent my knowing that she kept her lights burning all night. But why make a secret of it? That is what I can't understand! She has had a shock, and it has probably made her afraid of the dark, which she has never been before, and perhaps she looks upon it as a weakness to be ashamed of. Another unfortunate thing occurred this morning. May has lately been breakfasting in bed, but, as ill-luck would have it, to-day she got down-stairs before I did, and was already looking over the newspaper when I came into the room. Suddenly she started up, her eyes wild with terror, and then with a low cry fell fainting to the floor.

"Snatching up the paper to see what could have caused her such agitation, I was horrified to read that the man who was found murdered in our apartment house was now supposed to be Maurice Greywood. Imagine my feelings! As soon as she had recovered sufficiently to be questioned, I begged her to confide in me—her mother. But she assured me that she had told me everything, and that the man who had been killed was a perfect stranger to her and not Mr. Greywood. She insists that the two do not even look very much alike, as the deceased is much larger, coarser, and darker than the young artist. It was, of course, the greatest relief to know this. Had Greywood really been at the Rosemere on the evening she spent there, I should always have believed that they had met by appointment. 'Yes, I should; I know I should,' she repeated, as I shook my head in dissent.

"When I was ready to go to church, I was astonished to find May waiting for me in the hall. She was perfectly composed, but a crimson spot burned in either cheek and her eyes were unnaturally bright. I noticed, also, that she had taken great pains with her appearance, and had put on one of her prettiest dresses. I could not account in any way for the change in her behaviour. As we neared the village, she almost took my breath away by begging me to telegraph to Mr. Norman to ask him to come and stay with us! 'Telegraph him now!' I exclaimed. 'Yes,' she replied; 'I would like to see him. If we telegraph immediately, he could get here by five o'clock.' 'But why this hurry?' I asked. She flushed angrily, and kept repeating: 'I want to see him.' 'But, my child,' I remonstrated, 'I don't even know where Mr. Norman is. He certainly is not in town at this time of the year.' 'Telegraph to his town address, anyhow, and if he isn't there it doesn't matter,' she urged.—'But, May, what is the meaning of this change? The last time he came down here you wouldn't even see him. Do you now mean to encourage him?' 'No, no,' she asserted. 'Then I shall certainly not send him such a crazy message,' I said. 'If you don't, I will,' she insisted. We were now opposite the post office. She stopped and I saw that she was trembling, and that her eyes were full of tears. 'My darling,' I begged her, 'tell me the meaning of all this?' 'I wish to see Mr. Norman,' is all she would say. Now, I suppose you will think me very weak, but I sent that telegram. Fred, tell me, do you think the child is going insane?" and the poor mother burst into tears.

"Dear, dear lady, I am sure you are unnecessarily alarmed. If I could see May, I could judge better."

"Yes, yes," she interrupted, eagerly, "that is what I wish. I thought if you came to the house as a visitor you could give me your professional opinion about May without her knowing anything about it. The difficulty is, how can you get to us with your poor leg?"

"Nothing easier," I assured her. "I can hobble about now on crutches, and with a little help can get in and out of a carriage; so I will drive over to you immediately after lunch."

"Won't you come now and lunch with us?"

"No; at lunch we should all three have to be together, and I would rather see your daughter by herself."

"Very well, then," said Mrs. Derwent, and gathering up the folds of her soft silk gown she left me.

Early this afternoon I drove over to their place, and found both ladies sitting on the piazza. May greeted me very sweetly, but I at once noticed the peculiar tension of her manner, the feverish glitter of her eyes, the slight trembling of her lips, and did not wonder at her mother's anxiety. After a little desultory conversation, Mrs. Derwent left us alone. I doubt if the girl was even aware of her departure, or of the long pause which I allowed to follow it.

"May, Dr. Fortescue, whom you have read about in connection with the Rosemere tragedy, is a great friend of mine." She stared at me with horror. I felt a perfect brute, but as I believed it was for her good I persisted: "I think he saw you when you were in town." She staggered to her feet; I caught her to prevent her falling, and laid her gently on a divan. "Lie still," I commanded, looking her steadily in the eye. "Lie still, I tell you; you are in no condition to get up. Now, listen to me, May; I know you have had a shock, and your nerves are consequently thoroughly unstrung. Now, do you wish to be seriously ill, or do you not?" My quiet tones seemed to calm her. "Of course I don't want to be ill," she murmured. "Then you must not go on as you have been doing lately. Will you let your old playfellow doctor you a little? Will you promise to take some medicine I am going to send you? I must tell you that, unless you will do what I say, you will be delirious in a few hours." I thought that argument would fetch her.

"Yes, yes," she exclaimed. "What shall I do?" and she put her hand to her head and gazed about her helplessly.

"In the first place, you must go to bed immediately."

"I can't do that; Mr. Norman will be here in a few hours."

"Well, I can't help it. To bed you must go, and from what I hear of that young man he will be as anxious as anybody to have you do what is best for you."

"But—" she objected.—"There is no 'but.' Unless you at once do as I tell you, you will be down with brain fever."

"Very well, then," she meekly replied; "I will go to bed."

"That's a good girl. You must get a long night's rest, and if you are better in the morning I will let you see your friend. He'll wait, you know; I don't believe he will be in any hurry to leave, do you?" But she only frowned at my attempt at jocularity. I rang the bell and asked the butler to call Mrs. Derwent, to whom I gave full directions as to what I wanted done, and had the satisfaction of seeing May go up-stairs with her mother. I waited till the latter came down again, and then told her as gently as possible that her daughter was on the verge of brain fever, but that I hoped her excellent constitution might still save her from a severe illness.

The next question was, what to do with Norman.

May's positive belief that he was coming had proved contagious, and I found that we were both expecting him. I thought it would be best for me to meet him at the train, tell him of May's sudden illness and offer to put him up at our place for the night. Mrs. Derwent, after some hesitation, agreed to this plan. Norman turned up, as I knew he would. He is very quiet, and does not appear surprised either at his sudden invitation or at May's illness. He also seems to think it quite natural that he should stay in the neighbourhood till she is able to see him. He looks far from well himself, and is evidently worried to death about May. He has been out all the evening, and I suspect him of having been prowling around the Beloved's house.

Now tell me—what do you think is the meaning of all this? Is the body Maurice Greywood's, or is it not? If it is he—who killed him and why? If she—but I'll not believe it unless I also believe her to have had a sudden attack of acute mania—and that, of course, is possible, especially when we consider what a highly nervous state she is still in.

But if the dead man was really a stranger to her, as she asserts, why then does every mention of the murder cause her to become so excited? Why does she appear to be for ever watching for somebody? Why did she cry out in her sleep: "Oh, he's dead, he's dead!"? Again, the only reasonable explanation seems to be that her mind has become slightly unhinged. And if that is the case, what rôle does Norman play in this tragedy, and why did she insist on his being sent for? Above all, why does he consider it natural that she should have done so?

Now, knowing all this, can you advise me as to what I ought to do to help the poor girl?

I hear Norman coming in, so must end abruptly, although I have a lot more to say.

Affectionately yours,
FRED.

CHAPTER IX

W HILE these things had been happening in the country, my Sunday in town had been almost equally eventful.

I had not been surprised on receiving Fred's telegram the evening before to find that the name it contained was that of the young artist. Had he not already told me that Greywood was supposed to have been the favoured suitor? And, knowing May Derwent as I did, I had felt sure from the very first that she must have entertained the liveliest feelings of trust and liking—to say the least—for the man whom she permitted to visit her on that Tuesday evening. That the cur had not known enough to respect the privilege filled me with mingled feelings of rage and delight. Had he not offended my divinity there would have been no chance for me, and yet that he had dared to do so made me long to punish him.

But to do this I must first find him. His name did not appear either in the Social Register or the Directory, but I thought that by visiting the various studio buildings dotted over the city I should eventually find the one in which he lived.

So I got up bright and early the following morning, determined to begin my search at once. As I sat down to my breakfast with a hopeful heart and an excellent appetite, I little thought what a bomb-shell was contained in the papers lying so innocently beside my plate.

I had hardly read the terrible news before I was out of the house and on my way to Merritt's. Luckily, I found the detective at home, calmly eating his breakfast. He showed no signs of surprise at my early appearance, and invited me to share his meal with simple courtesy. As I had hurried off without stopping to eat anything, I thought that I had better do so, although I grudged the time spent in such a trifling pursuit, while so much hung in the balance and every minute might be precious.

"Well, Mr. Merritt," I exclaimed, "what is this fairytale about Greywood? I see from the papers that your people do not put much faith in the identification."

"We do, and we don't," he answered, "but it is not proved yet, and, while there is still some doubt about it, I thought it as well for the gentlemen of the press to be kept guessing a little longer."

"But what do *you* think? Surely, you do not believe the murdered man to be Greywood?" I urged.

"Doctor, I'm afraid I do."

"You do?" I cried.

"Yes."

"But when I saw you, on Friday, you were equally sure of Miss Derwent's innocence."

"Ah! that was Friday! Besides, I have not said that I believe the young lady guilty; I merely say that I believe Maurice Greywood, and not Allan Brown, to be the name of the victim."

"But, then, you must think that she killed him," I insisted.

"Not necessarily. Have you never thought of the possibility that Allan Derwent (for we will assume that he was the man whom you saw in her apartment) might be the murderer?"

"No," I confessed, "that had not occurred to me."

"But it ought to have, for of all the theories we have as yet entertained, this one is by far the most probable. You see," he continued, "you allow your judgment to be warped by your unwillingness to associate the young lady, even indirectly, with a crime."

"Perhaps so," I acknowledged.

"Now, I must tell you that, however innocent Miss Derwent may eventually prove to be, since my last talk with you I have become convinced that the murder was committed in her parlour, and nowhere else." Mr. Merritt spoke very earnestly, leaning across the table to watch the effect on me of what he was saying.

"Ah," I exclaimed angrily, "then you deceived me——"

"Gently, gently, young man; I don't deceive anybody. I told you that I wished the young lady well; so I do—that I believed in her innocence; I still do so. I said that the information I had received from you materially helped her case, which it most assuredly did. Had you withheld certain facts it would have been my duty—my painful duty, I acknowledge—to have arrested Miss Derwent last Saturday."

"But why?" I inquired.

"Because all the evidence pointed towards her, and because my belief in her innocence rested on no more solid foundation than what is called intuition, and intuition is a quicksand to build upon."

"But what was there to point to her except that a negro boy thought that the dead man resembled Greywood?"

"Ah, you acknowledge that her visitor was Mr. Greywood?"

"Yes, I grant you that, but what of it? I am convinced he has not been murdered."

"But why?" demanded the detective. "Now, listen to this. The body is identified by two people as Greywood's. Greywood disappears at about the same time that the crime was committed. We know that the corpse must have been hidden somewhere in the Rosemere for twenty-four hours. Where could it have been more easily secreted than in the Derwents' apartment, into which no outsider or servant entered? And lastly, it would have required two people to carry, even for a short distance, a body of its size and weight; but as the young lady was not alone, but had with her the man and woman whom you saw, this difficulty is also disposed of. From all this, I conclude that the Derwents' flat was the scene of the tragedy."

"But why should Greywood have been killed?" I asked. "What possible motive could there have been?"

"Oh, it is easy enough to imagine motives, although I do not guarantee having hit on the right one. But what do you think of this for a guess? Miss Derwent, who knows that her brother may any day be in need of a hiding-place, has given him the key to their back door. Coming to town, she meets Greywood, dines with him, and invites him to spend the evening with her (having some reason for supposing that her brother is safely out of the way). During this visit they have a violent quarrel, and, in the midst of it, young Derwent, who has come in through the kitchen, suddenly appears. Let us also presume that he is intoxicated. He discovers his sister alone with a man, who is unknown to him, and with whom she is engaged in a bitter dispute. The instinct to protect her rises within him. His eyes fall on a weapon, lying, let us suppose, on the parlour table. He seizes it, and in his drunken rage, staggers across the room and plunges it into Greywood's heart. What girl could be placed in a more terrible position? She is naturally forced to shield her brother. So she hits on a plan for diverting suspicion from him, which would have been successful, if Fate had not intervened in the most extraordinary way. You remember, that it came out that on Wednesday she went in and out of the building very frequently. During one of these many comings and goings, she manages to extract the key of the vacant apartment, to have it copied, and to return it without its absence being noticed. They then wait till the early hours of the morning before venturing to move the body, which they carry to the place where it was found. Unfortunately for them, they locked the dead man in, and in this way rendered their detection much more easy. For it limited the number of suspected persons to three—to the three people, in fact, who could have had the key in their possession, even for a short time. On returning to their own rooms, they discover that they have lost something of great importance. The young man searches for it long and vigorously. He does not find it——"

"How do you know he didn't find it?" I interrupted.

"Because *I* found it," asserted the detective triumphantly.

"Indeed! And what was it?"

"The handle—or, to be more accurate, the head—of the fatal weapon."

"Really!" I exclaimed; "you found it? Where?"

"It had fallen in between the dead man's trousers and the folds of his shirt."

"It must be pretty small, then."

"It is. Look at it," and he laid on the table a jewelled dagger-hilt about an inch and a half long.

"That!" I exclaimed contemptuously; "why, that is nothing but a toy."

"Not a toy," replied Mr. Merritt, "but an ornament. A useful ornament; for it is the head of one of those jewelled hat-pins that have been so fashionable of late. A dagger with the hilt encrusted with precious stones is quite a common design."

"Did you find the pin itself?" I asked.

"No, I did not," the detective answered regretfully.

"How do you account for the handle being where you found it?"

"I think that in all probability the pin was removed from the body immediately after it had done its work, and in doing so the head was wrenched off. During the excitement which followed no one noticed where it fell, and its loss was not discovered till the victim had been disposed of. Young Derwent evidently expected the place to be searched, which accounts for the care with which he tried to remove all traces of his presence, and his extreme anxiety to find this, which, he feared, if discovered on the premises, might prove a sure clue. Now, that theory hangs together pretty well, don't it?" wound up the detective.

Without answering him, I inquired: "And what do you mean to do now?"

"I'm afraid I shall have to arrest Miss Derwent, as we can find no trace of her two companions. By the way, it is as you supposed;—the man you saw leaving the building was no tradesman, so he is probably the person we want. I have, therefore, given his description to the police, and hope soon to have some news of him."

"So, Mr. Merritt, you would really arrest a girl on such flimsy evidence, and for a crime you do not believe her to have committed?" I inquired indignantly.

"As for the evidence, I think it is fairly complete," answered the detective, "and I would not arrest Miss Derwent if I were not convinced that she is implicated in this affair, and think that this is the surest way of getting hold of the precious couple. I can't allow a criminal to slip through my fingers for sentimental reasons, and every hour's delay renders their escape more possible. The girl may be innocent,—I believe she is; but that one of that trio is guilty I am perfectly sure."

"Are you, really?" I exclaimed. "Well, I am not, and, if you will listen to me for a few minutes, I think I can easily prove to you that you are wrong. For since Friday I, too, have thought of a new and interesting point in connection with this case." The detective looked indulgently at me.

"You seem to forget," I continued, "and of this fact I am quite certain, that the victim met his death while wholly or partly unconscious."

Merritt gave a slight start, and his face fell.

"The autopsy must have been made by this time. Did not the doctor find traces of alcohol or a drug?" I demanded.

"Yes," admitted the detective, "alcohol was found in large quantities."

"Now, Greywood had been dining quietly with a lady, and it is inconceivable that he could have been drunk, or that, being in that condition, she should not have noticed it, which she could not have done—otherwise she would certainly not have allowed him to go up-stairs with her."

"That is a good point," said the detective.

"Besides, the corpse bears every indication of prolonged dissipation. Now, no one has hinted that Greywood drank."

"No, but he may have done so, for all that," said Mr. Merritt.

"He could not have done so to the extent of leaving such traces after death without its being widely known," I asserted. "The dead man must have been an habitual drunkard, remember, and that the young artist certainly was not. No, if you persist in believing the murdered man to be Greywood, you must also believe that Miss Derwent lured him to her rooms, while he was so intoxicated as to be almost, if not quite helpless, and there, either killed him herself or allowed her brother to kill him. In the latter case, do you not think a lady's hat-pin rather a feeble weapon for a young desperado to select? And that that description can be applied to Allan Derwent, everything I have heard of him tends to show.

"On the other hand, let us consider for a moment the probability of the body being Allan Brown's. What do we find? When last seen he was already noticeably intoxicated, and what is there more likely than that the daughter of a saloon-keeper should have no scruples about offering him the means of becoming still more so? And please notice another thing. You told me yourself that Mrs. Atkins had spent the greater part of her life among a very fast lot—so that it is perfectly natural to find a man of the deceased's habits among her familiar associates. But what is more unlikely than that a girl brought up as Miss Derwent has been should go so much out of her way as to choose such a man for her friend? And then, again, remember how the two women behaved when confronted with the corpse.

"Miss Derwent walked calmly in and deliberately lifted her heavy veil, which could easily have hidden from us whatever emotions she may have felt. Lifts it, I say, before looking at the body. Does that look like guilt? And what does Mrs. Atkins do? She shows the greatest horror and agitation. Now, mind you, I do not infer from this that she killed the man, but I do say that it proves that the man was no stranger to her. And now I come to the hat-pin. You assume, because you find a certain thing, and I saw a search carried on, that the man was looking for the object you found. What reason have you for believing this, except that it fits in very prettily with your theory of the crime? None. You cannot trace the possession of such an ornament to Miss Derwent, can you?" The detective shook his head. "Ah! I thought not. And even if you did, what would it prove? You say yourself that the design is not an uncommon one."

"No, but it certainly would be considered a very remarkable coincidence, and one that would tell heavily against her," the detective replied.

"Yes, I suppose so; but we needn't cross that bridge till we come to it. As yet, you know nothing as to the ownership of the pin. But I want to call your attention to another point. If two people have identified the body as the young artist, so have two others recognised it as that of Allan Brown, and I assert that the two former are not as worthy of credence as the two latter."

"How so," inquired Mr. Merritt.

"In the first place, Jim was much less positive as to the supposed identity of the deceased than Joe was. You admit that; consequently, I consider Joe's word in this case better than Jim's, and Mrs. Atkins is certainly a more reliable witness than Mrs. Mulroy, an Irish charwoman, with all her national love of a sensational story."

"That is all very fine," said Mr. Merritt, "but Mrs. Atkins emphatically denied knowing the deceased."

"In words, yes; but don't you think this is one of the cases where actions speak louder than words? By the way, I gather from your still being willing to discuss the corpse's identity that you have not been able to trace this mysterious Brown?"

"You are right. The only thing we have found out is, that the berth on the Boston train which was bought in his name was never occupied."

"And yet, in the face of all this, you still think of arresting Miss Derwent; of blighting a girl's life in such a wanton manner?"

"Doctor, you're right; I may have been hasty. Mrs. Greywood, the young man's mother, arrives to-morrow, and her testimony will be decisive. Should the body not be that of her son (and you have almost convinced me that it is not), then Miss Derwent's affairs are of no further interest to me, and who she may, or may not, entertain in her apartment it is not my business to inquire."

After a little more desultory talk, I left him to his morning paper. I was now more than ever determined to do a little work in his line myself, and felt quite sure that talent of a superior order lay dormant within me. Only the great difficulty was to know where to begin. I must get nearer the scene of the tragedy, I concluded; I must cultivate McGorry and be able to prowl around the Rosemere undisturbed. What a triumph if I should discover the missing hat, for instance!

All this time I was sauntering idly up-town, and as I did so I fell in with a stream of people coming from the Roman Catholic Cathedral. Walking among them, I noticed a woman coming rapidly towards me, who smiled at me encouragingly, even from quite a distance. Her face seemed strangely familiar, although I was unable to place her. Where had I seen those flashing black eyes before? Ah! I had it,—Mme. Argot. She was alone, and as she came nearer I saw she not only recognised me, but that she was intending to stop and speak to me. I was considerably surprised, but slowed down also, and we were just opposite to each other when her husband suddenly stepped to her side. A moment before I could have sworn he was not in sight. It was quite uncanny. His wife started and glanced fearfully at him, then tossing her head defiantly she swept past me with a beaming bow. He took off his hat most respectfully, and his long sallow face remained as expressionless as a mask. But I was sure that his piercing black eyes looked at me with secret hostility. The whole incident only occupied a minute, but it left a deep impression upon me, and started me off on an entirely new train of thought. What had the detective said? The guilty person must have been able to procure, for some time, however short, the key to the vacant apartment. We only knew of three people who were in a position to have done this. Miss Derwent, the French butler—well, why not the French butler? Those eyes looked capable of anything. I was sure that his wife was afraid of him, for I was certain that she had meant to stop and speak to me, and had been prevented from doing so by his sudden appearance. But what could she have wished to say to me? And why that gleam of hatred in her husband's eye? I felt myself so innocent towards them both. In fact, I had not even thought of them since the eventful Thursday, and might easily have passed her by unnoticed if she had not been so eager to attract my attention. Well, it would be queer if I had tumbled on the solution of the Rosemere mystery!

As I was now almost opposite my club, I decided to drop in there before going in search of McGorry. There were hardly any people about, and when I entered the reading-room I found that it contained but one other person besides myself. The man was very intent upon his paper, but as I approached he raised his head, and I at once recognised Mr. Stuart. The very person, of all others, I most wanted to see. Fate was certainly in a kindly mood to-day, and I determined it should not be my fault if I did not make the most of the opportunity thus unexpectedly afforded me. So when I caught his eye I bowed, and walked boldly up to him. He answered my salutation politely, but coldly, and appeared anxious to return to his reading; but I was too full of my purpose to be put off by anything. I said: "Mr. Stuart, you have quite forgotten me, which is not at all surprising, as I only met you once before, and that time was not introduced to you."

He smiled distantly, and looked inquiringly at me through his single eye-glass.

"It was last Thursday at the Rosemere," I explained.

He appeared startled. I think the idea of my being a detective suggested itself to him, so I continued, reassuringly:

"My name is Fortescue, and I am a doctor. My office is *vis-à-vis* to your building, so, probably on account of my proximity, I was called in to see the victim, and have naturally become much interested in this very mysterious affair."

"Indeed!" he remarked.

This was not encouraging, but I persisted.

"A very remarkable case, isn't it?" I said, trying to appear at ease.

"A most unpleasant business," he replied curtly.

My obstinacy was now aroused, so I drew a chair up and sat down.

"Mr. Stuart, I hope you won't think me very impertinent if I ask you whether you have any reason to be dissatisfied with your two servants?"

He now looked thoroughly alarmed.

"No; why do you ask?"

"You probably know that the identity of the dead man has never been established?" I continued.

"On the contrary," interrupted Mr. Stuart, "I am just reading an account of how it has been ascertained that the body is that of a man called Greywood."

"Oh," I replied airily, "that is only a bit of yellow journalism. If you read to the end, you will find that they admit that the police place no credence in their story. I have just been talking to Mr. Merritt about it——"

"Merritt, the detective, you mean?"

"Yes," I answered.

"Well, he must be an interesting man. I should like to see him."

"Why, you have seen him," I said; "he was the short, clean-shaven man who stood beside me, and afterwards followed you out."

"Really!" he exclaimed; "I wish I had known that; I have always taken a great interest in the man. He has cleared up some pretty mysterious crimes."

"I am sure he would be only too delighted to meet you. He's quite a nice fellow, too, and terribly keen about this murder," I added, bringing the conversation back to the point I wanted discussed.

"Yes?" said Mr. Stuart. "Of course, I am interested in it, too; but I confess that to have a thing like that occur in a building where one lives is really most unpleasant. I have been pestered to death by reporters."

"Well, I assure you I am not one," I said, with a laugh; "but, all the same, I should like to ask you a few questions."

"What are they?" he cautiously inquired.

"Do your butler and his wife get along well together?"

"Why do you want to know?" he asked, in his turn. I told him what had just happened. He smiled.

"Oh, that doesn't mean anything. Celestin is insanely jealous of his wife, whom he regards as the most fascinating of her sex, and has a habit of watching her, I believe, so as to guard against a possible lover."

"Do they quarrel much?"

"Not lately, I am glad to say. About a year ago it got so bad that I was forced to tell them that if I heard them doing so again, I should dismiss them both."

"Dear me, was it as bad as that?"

"Why, yes. One evening, when I came home, I heard shrieks coming from the kitchen, and, on investigating, found Celestin busily engaged in chastising his wife!"

"Really?"

"Yes, and the funniest thing is, that she did not seem to mind it much, although she must have been black and blue from the beating he gave her. It was some trouble about a cousin, I believe; but, as they are both excellent servants, I thought it best not to inquire too particularly into the business."

"And have they been on amicable terms since then?"

"Oh, yes. And, curiously enough, their behaviour to each other is positively lover-like. Even in the old days, she would flirt and he would beat her, and then they would bill and coo for a month. At least, so I judged from the little I saw of them."

I was now anxious to be off, but he seemed to have overcome his aversion or distrust, and detained me for some time longer, discussing the tragedy.

When I reached the Rosemere, I found McGorry sitting in his private office, and remarkably glad to see me. I offered him a cigar, and we sat down to a comfortable smoke. At first, we talked of nothing but the murder, but at last I managed to bring the conversation around to gossip about the different people in the building. This was no easy matter, for the fellow considered it either impolitic or disloyal to discuss his tenants, but, luckily, when I broached the subject of the Argots, he unbosomed himself. He assured me that they were most objectionable people, and he couldn't see why Mr. Stuart wanted to employ Dagos, as he called them. He told me that the woman was always having men hanging around, and that her husband was very violent and jealous.

"But they have stopped quarrelling, I hear."

"Stopped, is it?" he exclaimed with fine scorn. "I suppose Mr. Stuart told you that. Little he knows about it. They darsn't make a noise when he's about.

But Argot's been terrible to her lately. Why, they made such a row that I had to go in there the other day and tell him if he didn't shut up I'd complain to Mr. Stuart. He glared at me, but they've been quieter since then. I guess she's a bad lot, and deserves what she gets, or else she wouldn't stand it."

"I say, McGorry, you have seen nothing of a straw hat, have you?"

"Lord! Hasn't Mr. Merritt been bothering me to death about that hat? No, I haven't found one."

That was all I could get out of him. Not much, but still something.

Returning to my office, I sat for a long time pondering over all I had seen and heard that morning, and the longer I thought the more likely did it seem that the corpse was that of some lover of Madame Argot's whom her husband had killed in an attack of jealous frenzy. I had never for a moment considered the possibility of the body being Greywood's, and Merritt thought the objections to its being that of the vanished Brown equally insurmountable. I was, therefore, forced to believe in the presence on that fatal Tuesday of yet another man. That he had not entered by the front door was certain; very well, then, he must have come in by the back one. Of course, that there should have been three people answering to the same description in the building at the time when the murder occurred seemed an incredible conglomeration of circumstances, but had not the detective himself suggested such a possibility? The most serious objections to the supposition that Argot had murdered the man were: first, the smallness of the wound, and, secondly, the distance of the place where the body was found from Stuart's apartment. The first difficulty I disposed of easily. Merritt had failed to convince me that a hat-pin had caused the fellow's death, and I thought it much more likely that the ornament found on the corpse was a simple bauble which had nothing to do with the tragedy. Now, a small stiletto—or, hold, I had it—a skewer! A skewer was a much more likely weapon than a hat-pin, anyhow, besides being just the sort of a thing a butler would find ready to his hand.

The next objection was more difficult to meet, yet it did not seem impossible that, having killed the man, Argot should, with his wife's connivance, have secreted him in one of the closets which his master never opened, and then (having procured a duplicate key) have carried the body, in the wee small hours of the morning, up the three flights of stairs, and laid it in the empty apartment.

Thoroughly satisfied with this theory, I went off to lunch.

CHAPTER X

T HAT very evening, as I was sitting quietly in my office, trying to divert my mind from the murder by reading, my boy came in and told me that there was a lady in the waiting-room who wanted to see me. There was something so peculiar about the way he imparted this very commonplace information that my curiosity was aroused; but I refrained from questioning him, and curtly bade him show the lady in.

When she appeared I was no longer surprised at his manner, for a more strange and melodramatic figure I have seldom seen, even on the stage. The woman was tall and draped, or rather shrouded, in a long, black cloak, and a thick black veil was drawn down over her face. Her costume, especially considering the excessive heat, and that the clock pointed to 9.15, was alone enough to excite comment; but to a singularity in dress she added an even greater singularity of manner. She entered the room hesitatingly, and paused near the threshold to glance apprehensively about her, as if fearing the presence of some hidden enemy. The woman must be mad, I thought, as I motioned her to a chair and sat down opposite to her.

With a theatrical gesture, she threw back her veil, and to my astonishment I recognised the handsome, rotund features of—Madame Argot! She smiled, evidently enjoying my bewilderment.

"Meestair Docteur, I no disturb you?" she inquired.

"Certainly not, madame; what can I do for you?"

"Ah, meestair," she whispered, looking towards the door, "I so afraid zat my 'usban' 'e come back and fin' me gone; 'e terribly angry!"

"Why should he be angry?" I asked.

"He no like me to speak viz you. He no vant me to show you zis," she answered, pointing mysteriously to her left shoulder.

"What is it that he doesn't want me to see?"

"I go show you," and, opening her dress, she disclosed two terrible bruises, each as large as the palm of my hand; "and zat is not all," she continued, and, as she turned round, I saw that a deep gash disfigured one of her shoulder-blades.

I was really shocked.

"How did this happen?" I inquired.

"Oh, I fall," she said, smiling coquettishly at me.

"A very queer fall," I muttered.

The wound was several days old and not serious, but, owing to neglect, had got into a very bad condition.

"Ah, zat is better," she exclaimed, with a sigh of relief, when I had thoroughly cleansed the cut. I was just preparing to bandage it up, when she stopped me.

"No, meestair; not zat! My 'usban', 'e see zat, 'e know I come here, and zen 'e angry. Ze vashin' and ze salve zey make me better!"

"But look here, my good woman," I exclaimed, indignantly; "do you mean to say that your husband is such a brute that he objects to your having your wound dressed—a wound that you got in such a peculiar way, too?"

Her manner changed instantly; she drew herself haughtily up, and began buttoning up her dress.

"My 'usban' 'e no brute; 'e verra nice man; 'e love' me verra much."

"Really!"

"Yes," she asserted, "'e love me much, *oh oui, je vous assure qu'il m'adore!*" and she tossed her head and looked at me through the thick lashes of her half-closed eyes; "'e man, you know, 'e sometime jealous," she continued, smiling, as if his jealousy were a feather in her cap.

"Well, Madame Argot; that cut should be looked after, and, as it is in such a place that you cannot properly attend to it yourself, you must come in here every day, and I will dress it for you. Your husband cannot carry his devotion so far as to object to your covering it with a clean piece of linen, so I advise you to do that."

"Alla right, meestair, and zank you verra much. I come again ven I can, ven my 'usban' 'e go out sometime," and, after carefully wrapping herself up again, she sallied forth with infinite precautions.

Of course, the woman is a silly fool, and eaten up with vanity, but she had been pretty roughly handled, and that she should consider such treatment a tribute to her charms, seemed to me perfectly incomprehensible.

After reading for some time longer, I decided to go to bed, and, therefore, went into the front room to turn the lights out. Having done so, I lingered near the window, for the temperature here was at least several degrees cooler than the room I had just left. Although it was still early, the street appeared to be completely deserted, not a footfall was to be heard. As I stood there, half hidden by the curtain, a queer muffled noise fell upon my ears. It seemed to come from outside, and I moved nearer to the window, so as to try and discover what it could be. As I did so, a white face, not a foot away, peered suddenly into mine. I was so startled that I fell back a step, and before I recovered myself the creature was gone. I rushed out into the hall, and, unfastening the front door as quickly as I could, dashed into the street. Not a soul was in sight! The slight delay had given the fellow a chance to escape. Who could it have been? I wondered. A burglar, tempted by my open window? Or Argot, perhaps? This latter supposition was much the more alarming. What if he had seen his wife come out of my office? I thought of the murdered man, and shuddered. Notwithstanding the heat, I shut and bolted the window, and, as an extra precaution, also locked the door which connected the front room with my office and bedroom. I had no mind to be the next victim of an insane man's jealousy. All night long I was haunted by that white face! More and more it appeared to me to resemble Argot, till at last I determined to see Mr. Merritt and ask him if we had not sufficient grounds to warrant the Frenchman's arrest.

But when the morning came, things looked very different. Fred's second letter (which I have inserted in the place where it rightly belongs in the development of this story) arrived, and the thought of May Derwent's illness put everything else out of my mind. I might as well confess at once, that with me it had been a case of love at first sight, and that from the day I saw her at the Rosemere the dearest wish of my heart was to have her for my wife. And now she was ill and another man—a man who also loved her—had been summoned by her to fill the place I coveted. The consciousness of *his* devotion would uphold her during her illness, and his company help to while away the weary hours of convalescence. And here was I, tied to my post, and forced to abandon the field to another without even a struggle. For I felt it would be little short of murder to desert my patients while the thermometer stood high in the nineties and most of the other doctors were out of town. But if I could not go to my lady, she should, at any rate, have something of mine to bear her company. Rushing out to a nearby florist's I bought out half his stock. Of course, my gift had to go to her anonymously, but, even so, it was a comfort to me to think that, perhaps, my roses might be chosen to brighten her sick room. At all events, they would serve to remind her that there were other men in the world who loved her besides the one who was with her at that moment.

The afternoon edition of the *New York Bugle* contained the announcement that Mrs. Greywood had arrived in town that morning, and, on being shown the body of the Rosemere victim, had emphatically denied that it was that of her son. She thinks that the latter has gone off cruising, which he has been expecting to do for some time past; and that, of course, would explain his not having been heard from. The possibility of May Derwent's having been, even indirectly implicated in the murder, was thus finally disposed of. But I had been so sure, from the very first, of the ultimate result of their investigations, that Mrs. Greywood's statement was hardly a relief to me. Of course, I was very glad that no detective would now have an excuse for prying into my darling's affairs. Otherwise, I was entirely indifferent to their suspicions.

But these various occurrences helped to obliterate the memory of the events of the previous night, and, as I had no time to hunt up the detective, I decided to think no more about my strange adventure.

I was rather late in leaving the hospital that afternoon, and when I reached home my boy told me that several patients were already waiting for me. I hurried into my office and sat down at my desk, on which a number of letters had accumulated. I was looking these over when I heard the door open, and, glancing up, my eyes fell upon—Argot! I stared at him for a moment in silence. Could this reserved and highly respectable person be my visitor of the night before? Never, I concluded. He stood respectfully near the door, till I motioned him to a seat. He sat gingerly down on the very edge of the chair, and, laying his hat on my desk, pulled out a handkerchief and mopped his forehead. I waited for him to begin, which he seemed to find some difficulty in doing. At last he said:

"Meestair, I come about a verra sad zing."

"Yes?" I inquired.

"You 'ave seen my vife?"

I did not answer at once; then, as I was uncertain how much he knew, I decided that it would be safest to confine myself to a bare nod.

"She is a verra fine woman, not?" he demanded, with visible pride.

"Very much so," I assented. What could he be leading up to, I wondered?

"But, helas," he continued, "she is a little—" here he touched his forehead significantly, while he gazed at me less keenly from under his bushy brows.

"Really, you surprise me," was all I said.

"She quite wild some time," he insisted.

"Indeed?"

"Yes; she do some strange zings; she verra good vife—sough—verra good cook." He paused.

"What are you telling me all this for? What do you want me to do about it?" I inquired.

"Eh bien, Meestair; it is because she vant to come to see you, and she like you to be sorry, so she 'ave t'rowed herself down and 'ave 'urt 'erself. She lika ze mens too much," he added, fiercely, while a malignant expression flitted across his face.

It no longer seemed to me impossible that this middle-aged butler and the apparition of the night before could be identical, and there and then I determined that in future a pistol should repose in the top drawer of my desk.

"Perhaps your wife is slightly hysterical," I suggested.

Now, for the first time, my eyes left his face, and happened to fall on his hat, which was lying brim upwards at my elbow. My astonishment, when I noticed that the initials A. B. were printed in large letters on the inner band, was so great that I could hardly control myself. I looked for the maker's name —Halstead, Chicago, I made out. Could this be the missing hat? It seemed incredible. Argot would never dare display so openly such a proof of his guilt! But if he were demented (which I firmly believed him to be) would not this flaunting of his crime be one of the things one might expect of an insane man? I had been so startled that it was some minutes before I dared raise my eyes, fearing that their expression would betray me. I have absolutely no idea what he was talking about during that time, but the next sentence I caught was: "She vill, she vill come, but you jus' say, nonsense, zat is nossing, and zen she go."

"Very well," I assured him, anxious to get rid of the fellow. "I quite understand;" and, rising from my chair, I dismissed him with a nod.

My office was still full of people, and I think that seeing those other patients was about the most difficult thing I ever did. But at last even that ordeal was over, and I was able to start out in search of the detective. I had a good deal of difficulty in finding him, and, after telephoning all over creation, at last met him accidentally, not far from the Rosemere. I was so excited that I hailed him from a long way off, pointing significantly the while to my hat. By Jove, you should have seen him sprint! I had no idea those short legs of his could make such good time. We met almost directly in front of my door.

"What is it?" he panted.

Without answering, I took him by the elbow and led him into the house. He sank exhausted into one of my office chairs.

74

"What's up?" he repeated.

"Well," I began slowly, for I meant to enjoy my small triumph to the full, "I only wanted to ask you if you have yet found the missing hat?"

"No; have you?"

"No; I can't say I have." His face fell perceptibly. "But I know where a straw hat bearing the name of a Chicago hatter, and with the initials, 'A. B.,' stamped on the inside band, can be found," I added.

"You don't say so? Where is it?" He spoke quietly, but I noticed that his eyes glistened.

"I don't quite know where it is at this moment, but when I last saw it, it was on this desk."

"On this desk, and you allowed it—" He paused, speechless with disgust.

"Certainly, I allowed it to be taken away, if that is what you mean. However, you can easily get it again. It is not far off. But, I assure you, I have no intention of appearing in the character of the corpse in another sensational tragedy."

"Who brought it here?" demanded Mr. Merritt.

"Well, do you think that Argot would be a likely person?" I asked.

"Argot!" He was evidently surprised.

"Yes, Argot." And I told him all that I had lately discovered about the couple, and of their separate visits to me. Neither did I fail to mention the strange apparition of the night before, which had caused me so much uneasiness.

He seemed much impressed, and stared gravely before him for some minutes.

"You are really not at all sure that the white face belonged to Argot, are you?"

"No," I acknowledged.

"Well, Doctor," he continued, after a slight pause, "it's a queer thing that, just as you have succeeded in persuading me that a hat-pin is hardly a masculine weapon, and that, therefore, I ought to look for a murderess, and not a murderer, you, on the other hand, should have come to the conclusion that a man is the perpetrator of this crime."

"Ah! but you see, Mr. Merritt, I don't believe the victim was killed by a hat-pin. I think he was pierced through the heart by a skewer, which, in a kitchen, Argot would have found under his hand."

"Well, Doctor, you may be right. Live and learn, I always say. I shall at once call on the Argots, and have a look at this hat."

"Don't you think you had better have him arrested, first, and question him afterwards? I am convinced he is insane, and likely to become violent at any moment; we don't want any more murders, you know."

"That is all very well, Doctor; but I can't have the fellow arrested till I have something to go on. The hat you saw may not be the one we want; or, again, Argot may have found it."

"Well, if you insist on bearding him, let me go with you."

"Certainly not. You are young, and—well, not uncalculated to arouse his marital jealousy, while I," patting his portly person, "am not likely to cause him any such anxieties. Even age and fat have their uses, sometimes."

"But he may try to cut your throat," I objected.

"One of my men will be just outside, and will probably get to me before he has quite finished me." He had risen, and stood with his hand on the door-knob.

"Look here, Doctor, I'd like to bet you that Argot is innocent, and that a woman, and a mighty pretty woman, too, is the guilty party."

"All right, Mr. Merritt; I'll take you. I bet you fifty dollars that a man committed this crime."

"Done!" exclaimed the detective, and, pulling out his pocket-book, he recorded the bet with great care. He looked at me for a moment longer with one of those quiet enigmatic smiles of his, and departed.

I watched him cross the street and enter the back door of the Rosemere. A moment afterwards a shabby-looking man came slouching along and stopped just outside, apparently absorbed in watching something in the gutter. The detective remained only a minute or so in the building, and when he came out he gave me a slight nod, which I interpreted as a sign that Argot was not at home. He took not the slightest notice of the tramp, and, turning north, trotted briskly up town.

As I watched him disappear, I wondered what made him so sure of the Frenchman's innocence, and I tried vainly to guess who the woman could be whom he now had in mind. Miss Derwent, I was glad to say, was out of the question. He himself had proved to me by the most convincing arguments that Mrs. Atkins could not be guilty. And who else was there to suspect? For the criminal must have been an inmate of the building. That was one of the few facts which the detective claimed was established beyond a doubt.

CHAPTER XI

A FTER my interview with the detective, I went out to visit some patients, and on my way home I met young Atkins, whom I had not seen since the preceding Thursday. Although we had met but once, he recognised me immediately, and greeted me most cordially. I was, however, shocked to see what havoc a short week had wrought in his looks. His face was drawn and pale, and he appeared nervous and ill at ease. Notwithstanding he had been walking in the opposite direction, he at once turned back, and we sauntered towards Madison Avenue together. Our chief topic of conversation was naturally the murder, and we both remarked how strange it was that the identity of the victim had not yet been established.

"I suppose," said Atkins, "that we shall now never know who the man was, for I hear he was buried yesterday."

"Oh, that doesn't at all follow," I assured him; "photographs have been taken of the corpse, and, if necessary, it can be exhumed at any time."

Was my imagination playing me a trick, or was the young fellow really troubled by this information? We had now reached my destination, and, as I held out my hand to bid him good-bye, I said: "I am afraid Mrs. Atkins must have such unpleasant associations with me that she will not care to have me recalled to her notice; otherwise I should ask you to remember me to her. I hope she is well, and has not suffered too much from this prolonged heat?"

"I fear she's not very well," he replied. "It seems to have upset her nerves a good deal to have a murder occur in the building."

"Yes, that is only natural. Wouldn't it be advisable to take her away from here for a short time?" I suggested.

"I only wish she'd go; but she's got some maggot in her head, and refuses to stir." He paused a moment and glanced almost timidly at me.

"Doctor," he burst out, "I wish you'd come and dine with us this evening. It would be a real kindness. Wife and I both have the blues, and you'd cheer us up no end."

I was rather taken aback by his eagerness. "I'm very sorry, I can't possibly do so to-night, for I've just promised to dine with an old friend, who is only in town for a short time."

"Well, if you can't come to-night, won't you come to-morrow?" he urged.

I hesitated a moment. On the one hand I was anxious to oblige Atkins, whom I liked, and quite curious to see his wife again, and fathom, if possible, the cause of the change in her husband; while, on the other hand, I felt some delicacy about invading a lady's home when I had reason to believe that my being there would not be agreeable to her, for I remembered that she had refused even to look at me on leaving the coroner's presence.

"If you are sure Mrs. Atkins would care to see me, I shall be delighted to accept your invitation."

"Why should she object to see you?" he demanded.

"There is really no reason," I hastened to explain; "only as you tell me your wife has been much upset by the murder, and is consequently rather nervous at present, I don't wish to inflict myself on her if there is the least danger that my company may recall that tragic occurrence too vividly to her."

Atkins gave me a long, penetrating look, but having apparently satisfied himself that I had given my real reason, he said:

"Nonsense, Doctor! Mrs. Atkins isn't as unreasonable as that. I'm sure she'll be glad to see you. Now, remember, we shall expect you at seven sharp to-morrow."

"All right," I called back to him.

I have given such a long account of this trifling incident, because for some time afterwards I could not get the young fellow's face out of my mind, and I kept imagining all sorts of possible, and impossible, reasons for his changed looks. Could it be that he suspected the murdered man to have been a friend of his wife's, and feared that she might have some guilty knowledge of his death?

As I realised how such a thought would torture him, I wanted to go at once and tell him how my first grave suspicions had been confirmed, till now I was fully convinced of Argot's guilt. But, fearing that some injudicious word might show him that I had guessed the cause of his anxiety, I refrained. That evening after dining quietly at the Club with an old school-fellow I walked slowly home, down Madison Avenue, which, with its long rows of houses, almost all of which were closed up for the summer, presented an extremely dreary aspect. Although it was barely nine o'clock, the streets in that part of the town were well nigh deserted, everyone who could do so having fled from the city. The night was extremely dark, damp and hot. As I was nearing my office, I observed that the back door of the Rosemere was being cautiously opened, and a woman's head, covered with a thick veil, peeped out. Madame

Argot, I thought, and so it proved. Having satisfied herself that her lord and master was not in sight, she darted across the street, and disappeared in my house. I hurried up, so as not to keep her waiting, and, as I did so, I fancied I heard some one running behind me. Turning quickly around, I detected nothing suspicious. The only person I could see was a very fat man, whom I had passed several blocks back. Was he nearer than he should have been? I couldn't tell. At any rate, he was still far enough away for it to be impossible to distinguish his features, but as I was sure that he was not Argot, I did not wait for him to come up with me. On entering the reception room, I found Madame, still heavily veiled, huddled up in a corner, where she thought she could not be seen from the street. I told her to go into the office and, approaching the window, I looked out. There was still nobody in sight except the fat man, and he had crossed over, and was ambling quietly along on the other side of the way. He was almost opposite now, and, after looking at him critically, I decided that it was too improbable that the running foot steps I had heard following me had been his. But whose were they, then? I trusted that the murder had not affected my nerves, also. At any rate, I decided to take the precaution of shutting and bolting the window, and of pulling down the blind, none of which things, during this hot weather, had I been in the habit of doing. But I did not intend to give that white-faced apparition, to whom I attributed the mysterious footsteps, the chance of falling upon me unaware, especially not while Madame Argot was on the premises.

"Well, how goes it?" I inquired, when I at last rejoined her.

"Oh, much, much better, Meestair."

I saw, indeed, when I examined the cut, that it was healing splendidly.

"Meestair Docteur," she began as soon as I had settled down to dress her wound, "'usban' 'e come 'ere zis mornin'?"

"Yes," I assented.

"Ana what 'e say, Meestair?"

"Oh, I can't tell you that! Yon wouldn't like me to repeat to him all that you say to me, would you?"

"No; but zen, me is different; I know 'e say zat me a bad 'oman; I know, I know!"

"Indeed, he said nothing of the sort, and if you don't keep a little quieter, I shall really not be able to do my work properly."

"Oh, pardon; I vill be so good."

"By the way," I inquired, "did Mr. Merritt call on you to-day?"

"Ah! you means ze gentleman vat I see, ven I go ze dead man's?"

"Yes."

"He a big policeman, not?" she asked.

"Well, not a very big one," I answered, with a smile, "but he does a good deal of important work for the police."

"Ah, yes. Important, *oui*," she nodded. "Vy 'e come see my 'usban'? Do you know? I not know; my 'usban', 'e not know, eizer."

"He didn't see your husband, then?"

"No; Argot, he not in."

"Well, I think Mr. Merritt is looking for a hat containing the initials, A. B., and he wanted to ask your husband if he had found it, by any chance."

She started up quite regardless of her wound.

"Ah, *par example, oui*! Yes, indeed," she exclaimed, vehemently.

"Your husband has found such a hat?"

"Yes, yes; I tell you. 'e make *une* scenes about zat 'at!" she burst out, angrily.

"But why?" I asked. "Why should he make a scene about it?"

"Ah!" she said, tossing her head coquettishly, though real annoyance still lingered in her voice, "'e say it is ze 'at of my lover!"

"Really? Have you a lover whose initials are A. B.?"

"I 'ave no lover at all, Meestair! but I 'ave a cousin whose names begin vis zose letters."

"I see; but how did your husband happen to get his hat?"

"I not know; Argot 'e come in von evenin'——"

"What evening?" I interrupted.

"Tuesday evening, las' veek—" I suppose my face betrayed my excitement, for she stopped and asked, anxiously: "Vat is ze matter?"

"Nothing, nothing! go on; I am merely much interested in your story. Well, what happened on Tuesday?"

"Vell, Meestair," she resumed, "my 'usban' 'e go out to ze restaurant vere ze Frenchmens zey go play cards. Zen my cousin, M. Andrè Besnard, 'e come to call. My 'usban' 'e not zere, but I say, sit down; perhaps Argot 'e come in. My cousin 'e live in Chicago; 'e never seen my 'usban'; 'e not know 'e jealous. So 'e stay, ana 'e stay, an ve talks of France, ven ve vas chil'ren, and I forgets ze time, till I 'ears ze bell vat my 'usban' 'e ring, ana I looks at ze clocks an I see it say eleven. Zen I frightened. I know Argot dreadful angry if 'e fin' a man so late vis me. So I say, go avay, quick; my 'usban' 'e jealous; 'e no believe you my cousin. Go up ze stairs an' 'ide on ze next floor. Ven my 'usban' 'e come in, I shut ze kitchen door, and zen you can come down and go out. All vould 'ave been vell if 'e done zis, but zat imbecile 'e peeped over ze bannisters ven my 'usban' come in. But my 'usban' not quite sure 'e see somebody, so 'e say nossing, but ven I shut ze kitchen door 'e sit near it an' listen, and in a few minutes I 'ears creek, creek, an' 'e 'ears it, too; an' 'e jumps up, and I jumps up, for I afraid 'e kill my cousin; 'e look so angry. An' I puts my arms quite around 'im an' 'e fights, but I hold on, an' 'e falls vis me, an' so I got my bruises; but I no care, for I 'ears ze front door slam, so I knows Andrè is safe. In a minute my 'usban' he up and rushes out, an' me too; but ven I see Andrè is gone, I come back, but Argot 'e not come back."

"Your husband did not come back, you say?"

"No; 'e stay looking for Andrè——"

"How long was it before he came in again?"

"Ah! I not know," she exclaimed, impatiently, "'alf an hour, vone hour; me get tired an' I go to bed. Ven Argot 'e come in 'e terribly angry; 'e storm; 'e rage; 'e say, zat vas your lover; I say, no; zat vas nobody I knows. But hélas, I am unfortunate, for 'e find Andrè's card vat 'e left, for Andrè quite ze gentleman; zen, I sink, 'e have a fit; 'e swear 'e kill Andrè. But 'e not know vere Andrè is, because zere is no address on ze cards, but I know vere 'e is, for Andrè 'e told me. So ze next mornin' I writes to my cousin an' tell 'im my 'usban' 'e come for to kill 'im. But Argot 'e go out every day to try an' fin' 'im. And 'e not fin' im," she wound up, triumphantly, "because a friend of mine she tell me zat Andrè 'ave left New York an' 'ave gone back to Chicago."

"Did your cousin look much like the corpse?"

"Ah, but not at all. My cousin 'e little man vid no beard, for 'e is a vaitor."

"And you are sure your husband did not know him by sight."

"But certain," she asserted, vehemently.

"And you have no idea how your husband got hold of his hat?"

"No, Meestair, for I t'ought zat Andrè 'e took 'is 'at. An' Argot 'e say nossing about it till vone day——"

"What day?" I interrupted, again.

"Oh! vat zat matter? Thursday or Friday of last veek, I sinks. Vell, I come into the kitchen and zere is my 'usban' vis zat 'at. An' 'e glares at me. I no understand; I say, Vat you got? Vy don't you sit down, an' take off your at? 'e say, it is not my 'at; it 'as A. B. inside it, an' I vill vear it till I can bring you ze 'ead of zis A. B.; zis charming cousin whom you love so much. Yes! vait only, an' you shall have it, an' zen you shall vatch it rot!! And you dare say nossing—nossing,—for you be afraid ve gets 'anged for murder. But *I* say it no murder to kill ze lover of my vife. I say, Argot, you crazy; vere you get zat 'at? 'e say, Never min'."

"Aren't you afraid to stay with your husband? In one of his fits of insane jealousy he might kill you."

"Oh, no," she assured me; "'e beat me, but 'e no kill me; 'e love me too much. It make 'im too sad if I die. But tell me vy Andrè 'e send ze police for 'is 'at?"

Before I could answer her, I heard a crash in the hall, and two voices raised in vehement altercation. One of the voices belonged to my boy; the other, I didn't recognise.

"My 'usban'," whispered Madame Argot; "'e kill you."

She was as pale as death, and trembling with terror.

"No, you don't, sir; no, you don't," I heard the boy say. "Nobody goes into the Doctor's office, without being announced, while I'm here."

I rushed to the door leading into the hall, and had only just time to turn the key before a heavy mass was hurled against it. Luckily, the door was pretty solid, but it couldn't stand many such onslaughts. Quickly locking the other one, which opened into the waiting-room, I turned back to Madame Argot. What was to be done with her? For I was far from sharing her belief in her own safety. My office has only one other means of exit, as you know. This is a third door leading to my bed-room and bath-room. I decided at once that it was useless trying to hide Madame in either of these places. Any moment the door might give way before her husband's insane strength, and, then, it would infuriate him still more to find his wife in such a compromising position. No, the window, which opened on a small court, was our only hope. It was not a big drop to the ground, and, once there, she could easily make her way to the street, through the janitor's apartment. Without a word, I seized her and dragged her to the window.

"Put your feet out," I whispered; "give me your hands, and now let yourself go. It won't hurt you, and you will be able to escape through the basement."

"I cannot; I am afraid," she murmured, drawing back.

A pistol shot rang out, followed by the sound of splintering wood. I had no time to turn around, and see what had happened.

"Jump at once," I commanded.

She obeyed, almost unconscious from fear. She was pretty heavy, and very nearly had me out, too, but I managed to draw back, although the exertion was such that my arms ached for several hours afterwards. I stopped a moment to close the window partly, fearing that if I left it wide open, it might attract the madman's attention, and that he would be after her before she had time to get to a place of safety.

Turning back into the room, I saw that a bullet had pierced one of the panels of the door around which the fight seemed to be centred. A minute more, and it would give way. I rushed to the other one, and, quickly unlocking it, dashed through the waiting room, and caught the lunatic in the rear. With a bound, I was upon him, my two hands encircling his throat.

"Stand clear of that pistol!" I shouted, as Argot (for it was indeed he) tried to fire over his shoulder. A young man I had not seen before sprang forward, and, seizing his arm, bent it back till it caused a yell of pain and the pistol fell from the madman's grasp. At this juncture the janitor appeared, and the four of us had little difficulty in overpowering the fellow, although he still fought like a demon. As soon as he was safely bound, I sent my boy to telephone for an ambulance. I now observed, for the first time, that Argot had evidently tried to disguise himself. An enormous pillow, stuffed inside his trousers, and several towels, wound around his shoulders, gave him the appearance of extreme obesity. So, after all, he had been the fat man, and the running footsteps had been his. Well, I was glad that one mystery, at least, was cleared up.

The young stranger, whose opportune appearance had, in all probability, saved my life, still knelt beside the prostrate man, and he and I, together, succeeded in preventing him from breaking his bonds during one of his many paroxysms of frenzy.

"Thank you very much for your timely assistance," I said; "you are a brave man."

"Oh, not at all," he replied; "I am on duty here; I've been shadowing this man all the evening."

We had an awful job getting Argot into the ambulance, and I confess I never felt more relieved in my life than when I saw him safely locked up in a padded cell.

As I was coming away from the hospital, I met Merritt hurrying towards it.

"Hello!" he called out; "is it all over?"

"Yes; he's locked up, if that's what you mean."

"Well, Doctor, you've had a pretty lively time of it, my man tells me."

"It's entirely owing to your forethought, in having Argot immediately watched, that some of us are alive at present."

"You don't say; well, let's have a drink to celebrate the occasion. You look a little white around the gills, Doctor."

After tossing down my second bracer, I said: "Well, Mr. Merritt, how do you feel about your bet now?"

"Oh, all right," he answered, with a twinkle in his eye.

I stared at him in bewilderment. Then, remembering that of course he had not yet heard Madame's story, I proceeded at once to impart it to him.

"Very curious," was the only comment he made.

"But, look here, Mr. Merritt; what more do you want to convince you of the Frenchman's guilt?"

"Proofs; that's all," he replied cheerfully.

"But what further proof do you need? Here you have a man who is undoubtedly insane, who is furthermore an inmate of the Rosemere, and who, on Tuesday evening, went out with the avowed intention of killing his supposed rival; and, to cap the climax, the victim's hat is found in his possession. And yet, you have doubts!"

The detective only smiled quietly.

"By the way," he said, "I must go to the hospital, and get that hat before it disappears again."

I started.

"It didn't occur to me before, but when we put him into the ambulance, he was bareheaded," I confessed.

Merritt uttered an exclamation of impatience.

"We'll go to your place, then; it must be there. When you saw him in the street, he had on a hat similar to the one we are looking for, didn't he?"

"Yes."

"Then it's probably somewhere in your hall. That you shouldn't have noticed its absence does not surprise me so much, but that my man should have overlooked an article of such importance, does astonish me. It's his business to look after just such details."

When we reached the house we had to fight our way through a crowd of reporters, but in the hall, sure enough, we found the hat. Merritt positively pounced on it, and, taking it into my office, examined it carefully.

"What do you think of it?" I at last asked.

"I'm not yet prepared to say, Doctor; besides, you and I are now playing on different sides of the fence—of that $50, in other words, and till I can produce my pretty criminal, mum's the word."

"When will that be?"

"Let me see," replied the detective; "to-day is Tuesday. What do you say to this day week? If I haven't been able to prove my case before then, I will acknowledge myself in the wrong and hand you the $50."

"That suits me," I said.

I am ashamed to say that all this time I had forgotten about poor Madame. Having remembered her, I went to her at once, and found her violently hysterical and attended by several well-meaning, if helpless, Irish women, who listened to her voluble French with awe, not unmixed with distrust. I at last succeeded in calming her, but I was glad her master was spending several days out of town, for I could imagine nothing more distasteful to that correct gentleman than all this noise and notoriety. I was afraid that if he heard that more reporters were awaiting his return, he would not come back at all.

CHAPTER XII

BEVERLEY, L. I.,
Monday, August 15.

DEAR CHARLEY:

My leg is worse. Won't you run down here and have a look at it? I also want your advice about May Derwent.

Aff. yours,
FRED.

When I received this note early on Tuesday morning, I at once made arrangements for a short absence. Now that duty, and not inclination alone, called me elsewhere, I had no scruples about leaving New York; and when, a few hours later, after visiting my most urgent cases, I found myself on a train bound for Beverley, I blessed Fred's leg, which had procured me this unexpected little holiday. What a relief it was to leave the dust and the noise of the city behind, and to feast my eyes once more on the sight of fields and trees.

On arriving at my destination, I drove immediately to the Cowper's cottage. I found Fred in bed, with his leg a good deal swollen. His anxiety to go to the Derwents had tempted him to use it before it was sufficiently strong; consequently, he had strained it, and would now be laid up with it for some time longer.

"Well, Charley," he said, when I had finished replacing the bandages, "I don't suppose you are very sorry to be in this part of the world, eh? My leg did you a good turn, didn't it?"

I assented, curtly, for, although I agreed with him from the bottom of my heart, I didn't mean to be chaffed on a certain subject, even by him.

In order, probably, to tease me, he made no further allusion to the other object of my visit, so that I was, at last, forced to broach the subject myself.

"Oh, May? She's really much better. There is no doubt of it. I think the idea of brain fever thoroughly frightened her, for now she meekly obeys orders, and takes any medicine I prescribe without a murmur."

"Well, but then why did you write that you wished to consult me about her?"

"Because, Charley," he replied, laying aside his previously flippant manner, "although her general health has greatly improved, I can't say as much for her nervous condition. The latter seems to me so unsatisfactory that I am beginning to believe that Mrs. Derwent was not far wrong when she suggested that her daughter might be slightly demented."

I felt myself grow cold, notwithstanding the heat of the day. Then, remembering the quiet and collected way she had behaved under circumstances as trying as any I could imagine a girl's being placed in, I took courage again. May was not insane. I would not believe it.

"At all events," continued Fred, "I felt that she should not be left without medical care, and, as I can't get out to see her, and as she detests the only other doctor in the place, I suggested to Mrs. Derwent that she should consult you. Being a friend of mine, ostensibly here on a simple visit, it would be the most natural thing in the world for you to go over to their place, and you could thus see May, and judge of her condition without her knowing that she was under observation."

"That's well. It is always best to see a nervous patient off guard, if possible. Now, tell me all the particulars of the case."

When he had done this, I could not refrain from asking whether Norman was still there.

"Certainly! And seems likely to remain indefinitely."

"Really?"

"Yes! I forgot to tell you that May begged to be allowed to see him yesterday. As she was able to get up, and lie on the sofa, I consented, for I feared a refusal would agitate her too much. I only stipulated that he should not remain with her over half an hour. What occurred during this meeting, of course, I don't know. But May experienced no bad effects. On the contrary, her mother writes that she has seemed calmer and more cheerful ever since."

"They are probably engaged. Don't you think so?" And as I put the question, I knew that if the answer were affirmative my chance of happiness was gone for ever.

"I don't believe it," he answered, "for after his interview with May, Norman spent the rest of the day sunk in the deepest gloom. He ate scarcely anything, and when forced to remain in the house (feeling, I suppose, that politeness demanded that he should give us at any rate a little of his society) he moved restlessly from one seat to another. Several times he tried to pull himself together and to join in the conversation, but it was no use; notwithstanding all his efforts he would soon relapse into his former state of feverish unrest. Now, that doesn't look like the behaviour of a happy lover, does it?

"Since he has been here he has spent most of his time prowling about the Derwents' house, and as Alice was leaving their place yesterday evening she caught a glimpse of him hiding behind a clump of bushes just outside their gate. At least, she is almost sure that it was he, but was so afraid it would embarrass him to be caught playing sentinel that, after a cursory glance in his direction, she passed discreetly by. Afterwards it occurred to her that she should have made certain of his identity, for the man she saw may have been some questionable character. We are not sure that May's extreme nervousness is not due to the fact that she is being persecuted by some unscrupulous person, her brother, for instance. You know I have always believed that he was in some way connected with her illness."

"I know you have."

"But to return to Norman," continued Fred. "I not only suspect him of haunting her door by day, but of spending a good part of the night there. At any rate, I used to hear him creeping in and out of the house at all sorts of unusual hours. The first night I took him for a burglar, and showed what I consider true courage by starting out after him with an empty pistol and—a crutch!"

"I don't think that anything you have told me, however, is at all incompatible with his being Miss Derwent's accepted suitor. His distress is probably due to anxiety about her health." I said this, hoping he would contradict me.

Whether he would have done so or not I shall never know, for at that point our conversation was interrupted by the entrance of his sister; and as it had been previously arranged that she was to drive me over to the Derwents, we started off at once.

At last I was to see my lady again! It seemed too good to be true.

Having given our names to the butler, we were ushered into a large drawing-room, redolent with flowers. So this was May's home.

I glanced eagerly about. These chairs had held her slight form; at that desk she had written, and these rugs had felt the impress of her little feet. A book lay near me on a small table. I passed my fingers lovingly over it. This contact with an object she must often have touched gave me an extraordinary pleasure,—a pleasure so great as to make me forget everything else,—and I started guiltily, and tried to lay the book down unobserved, when a tall, grey-haired lady stepped from the veranda into the room.

Mrs. Derwent greeted Miss Cowper affectionately, and welcomed me with quiet grace.

"Fred has told me so much about you, Dr. Fortescue, that I am very glad to meet you at last."

Then, turning to Alice Cowper, she said: "May wants very much to see you. She is lying in a hammock on the piazza, where it is much cooler than here. Dr. Fortescue and I will join you girls later."

"You have been told of my daughter's condition?" she inquired, as soon as we were alone.

"Yes. I hear, however, that there has been a marked improvement since Sunday."

"There was a great improvement. She seemed much less nervous yesterday, but to-day she has had another of her attacks."

"I am sorry to hear that. Do you know what brought this one on?"

"Yes. It was reading in the paper of the Frenchman's assault on you!"

"But I don't understand why that should have affected her."

"You will forgive my saying so, Doctor—neither do I, although I am extremely glad that you escaped from that madman unhurt."

She looked at me for a moment in silence, then said: "When Fred advised me to consult you about my daughter's health, I knew immediately that I had heard your name before, but could not remember in what connection I had heard it mentioned. In fact, it was not until I read in the *Bugle* that the man who was supposed to have committed the Rosemere murder had, last night, attempted to kill you that I realized that you were the young doctor whom my daughter had told me about. You were present when she was made to give an account of herself to the coroner, were you not?"

"Yes, but I trust that my slight association with that affair will make no difference."

She again interrupted me: "It makes the greatest difference, I assure you. As you are aware of the exact nature of the shock she has sustained, I am spared the painful necessity of informing a stranger of her escapade. We are naturally anxious that the fact of her having been in the building at the time of the murder should be known to as few people as possible. I am, therefore, very grateful to you for not mentioning the matter, even to Fred. Although I have been obliged to confide in him myself, I think that your not having done so indicates rare discretion on your part."

I bowed.

"You may rely on me," I said. "I have the greatest respect and admiration for Miss Derwent, and would be most unwilling to say anything which might lay her open to misconstruction."

"Thank you. Now, Doctor, you know exactly what occurred. You are consequently better able than any one else to judge whether what she has been through is in itself enough to account for her present illness."

"She is still very nervous?"

"Incredibly so. She cannot bear to be left alone a minute."

"And you know of no reason for this nervousness other than her experience at the Rosemere?"

"None."

"May I ask how the news of the butler's attack on me affected her?" How sweet to think that she had cared at all!

"Very strangely," replied Mrs. Derwent. "After reading the account of it she fainted, and it was quite an hour before she recovered consciousness. Since then she has expressed the greatest desire to go to New York, but will give no reason for this absurd whim. Mr. Norman was also much upset by the thought of the danger you had incurred."

"Mr. Norman! But I don't know him!"

"So he told me. To be able to feel so keenly for a stranger shows an extraordinary sensibility, does it not?"

She looked at me keenly.

"It does, indeed! It is most inexplicable!"

"I don't know whether Fred has told you that since my daughter was taken ill on Sunday she cannot bear to have Mr. Norman out of her sight. He has been here all day, and now she insists on his leaving the Cowpers and staying with us altogether. Her behaviour is incomprehensible."

This was pleasant news for me!

"Surely this desire for his society can mean but one thing?"

"Of course, you think that she must care for him, but I am quite sure that she does not."

"Really?" I could hardly keep the note of pleasure out of my voice.

"If she were in love with him I should consider her conduct quite normal. But it is the fact of her indifference that makes it so very curious."

"You are sure this indifference is real and not assumed?"

"Quite sure," replied Mrs. Derwent. "She tries to hide it, but I can see that his attentions are most unwelcome to her. If he happens, in handing her something, to touch her accidentally, she visibly shrinks from him. Oh, Mr. Norman has noticed this as well as I have, and it hurts him."

"And yet she cannot bear him out of her sight, you say?"

"Exactly. As long as he is within call she is quiet and contented, and in his absence she fidgets. And yet she does not care to talk to him, and does so with an effort that is perfectly apparent to me. The poor fellow is pathetically in love, and I can see that he suffers keenly from her indifference."

"I suppose he expects his patient devotion to win the day in the end."

"I don't think he does. I felt it my duty in the face of May's behaviour—which is unusual, to say the least—to tell him that I didn't believe she cared for him or meant to marry him. 'I quite understand that,' was all he answered. But why he does not expect her to do so, is what I should like to know. As she evidently can't live without him, I don't see why she won't live with him.

"But now, Dr. Fortescue," added Mrs. Derwent, rising to leave the room, "let us go to my daughter. She is prepared to see you. But your visit is purely social, remember."

A curtain of honeysuckle and roses protected one end of the piazza from the rays of an August sun, and it was in this scented nook, amid surroundings whose peace and beauty contrasted strangely with those of our first meeting, that I at last saw May Derwent again. She lay in a hammock, her golden head supported by a pile of be-ruffled cushions, and with one small slipper peeping from under her voluminous skirts. At our approach, however, she sprang to her feet, and came forward to meet us. I had thought and dreamt of her for six long weary days and nights, and yet, now that she stood before me, dressed in a trailing, white gown of some soft material, slightly opened at the neck and revealing her strong, white, young throat, her firm, rounded arms bare to the elbow, and with one superb rose (I devoutly hoped it was one of those I had sent her) as her only ornament, she made a picture of such surpassing loveliness as fairly to take my breath away. I had been doubtful as to how she would receive me, so that when she smilingly held out her hand, I felt a great weight roll off my heart. Her manner was perfectly composed, much more so than mine in fact. A beautiful blush alone betrayed her embarrassment at meeting me.

"Why, Dr. Fortescue," exclaimed Alice Cowper, "you never told me that you knew May."

"Our previous acquaintance was so slight that I did not expect Miss

Derwent to remember me." I answered evasively, wondering, as I did so, whether May had confided to her friend where and when it was that we had met.

"I want to congratulate you, Doctor," said Miss Derwent, changing the conversation abruptly, "on your recent escape."

"From the madman, you mean? It was a close shave, I assure you. For several minutes I was within nodding distance of St. Peter."

"How dreadful! But why was the fellow not locked up long before this?"

"I did all I could to have him put under restraint. Several days ago I told a detective that I was sure not only that Argot was insane, but that he had committed the Rosemere murder. But he wouldn't listen to me, and I came very near having to pay with my life for his pig-headedness. Every one has now come round to my way of thinking except this same detective, who still insists that the butler is innocent."

Now that the blush had faded from her cheek, I realised that she was indeed looking wretchedly pale and thin, and as she leaned eagerly forward I was shocked to see how her lips twitched and her hands trembled.

"So it was you who first put the police on the Frenchman's tracks?" she demanded.

"Yes. But you must remember that the success my first attempt at detective work has met with is largely due to the exceptional opportunities I have had for investigating this case. You may have noticed that no hat was found with the corpse and the police have therefore been searching everywhere for one that could reasonably be supposed to have belonged to the murdered man. Now, I may tell you, although I must ask you not to mention it, as the police do not yet wish that the fact become known, that it was I who found this missing hat in Argot's possession. But I can't boast much of my discovery, because the man brought it into my office himself. All I really did was to keep my eyes open, you see." I tried to speak modestly, for I was conscious of a secret pride in my achievement.

"I really cannot see why you should have taken upon yourself to play the detective!"

I was so startled by May's sudden attack on me that for a moment I remained speechless. Luckily, Mrs. Derwent saved me from the necessity of replying, by rising from her chair. Slipping her arm through Miss Cowper's, she said—casting a significant glance at me: "We will leave these people to quarrel over the pros and cons of amateur work, and you and I will go and see what Mr. Norman is doing over there in that arbour all by himself."

Fred had mentioned that at times May seemed alarmingly oblivious to what was going on around her, and I now noticed with profound anxiety that she appeared entirely unconscious of the departure of her mother and friend.

"Just suppose for a moment that this man Argot," she went on, as if our conversation had not been interrupted, "is innocent, and yet owing to an unfortunate combination of circumstances, is unable to prove himself so. Who should be held responsible for his death but you, Dr. Fortescue! Had you not meddled with what did not concern you, no one would have thought of suspecting this wretched Frenchman! You acknowledge that yourself?"

"But, my dear Miss Derwent, why do you take for granted that the fellow is innocent?—although, in his present state of health, it really does not make much difference whether he is or not. In this country we do not punish maniacs, even homicidal ones. We only shut them up till they are well again. I think, however, that you take a morbid view of the whole question. Of course, justice sometimes miscarries, but not often, and to one person who is unjustly convicted, there are hundreds of criminals who escape punishment. As with everything else—medicine, for instance; you do your best, take every precaution, and then, if you make a mistake, the only thing to do is not to blame yourself too severely for the consequences."

"I quite agree with you," she said, "when to take a risk is part of your business. But is it not foolhardy to do so when there is no call for it?—when your inexperience renders you much more likely to commit some fatal error? What would you say if I tried to perform an operation, for instance?"

She was working herself into such a state of excitement that I became alarmed; so, abruptly changing the subject, I inquired after her health. She professed to feel perfectly well (which I doubted). Still I did not take as serious a view of her case as Fred had done; for I knew—what both he and Mrs. Derwent ignored—that while in town the poor girl had been through various trying experiences. During that time she had not only been forced to break with Greywood, to whom I was sure she had been engaged, but an entanglement, the nature of which I did not know, had induced her to give shelter secretly, and at night, to two people of undoubtedly questionable character. The shock of the murder was but a climax to all this. No wonder that my poor darling—her heart bleeding from the uprooting of an affection which, however unworthy the object of it had proved, must still have been difficult to eradicate; her mind harassed by the fear of impending disgrace to some person whom I must believe her to be very intimately concerned with; her nerves shaken by the horror of a murder under her very roof—should return to the haven of her home in a state bordering on brain fever. That she had not succumbed argued well for her constitution, I thought.

"Fred is quite worried about you, and asked me to beg you to take great care of yourself," I ventured to say.

"What nonsense! What I need is a little change. I should be all right if I could get away from here."

"This part of the world *is* pretty hot, I acknowledge. A trip to Maine or Canada would, no doubt, do you a lot of good."

"But I don't want to go to Maine or Canada—I want to go to New York."

"To New York?"

"Yes, why not? I find the country dull, and am longing for a glimpse of the city."

"But the heat in town is insufferable, and there is nothing going on there," I reminded her.

"Roof gardens are always amusing, and when the heat gets to a certain point, it is equally unbearable everywhere."

I begged to differ.

"At all events, I want to go there, and my wishing to do so should be enough for you. O Doctor, make Fred persuade Mamma to take me. As they both insist that I am ill, I don't see why they won't let me indulge this whim."

"They think that it would be very bad for you."

"Oh, it never does one any harm to do what one likes."

"What a delightful theory!"

"You will try and persuade Mamma and Fred to allow me to go to New York, won't you? You are a doctor; they would listen to you."

I glanced down into her beseeching blue eyes, then looked hastily away.

The temptation to allow her to do as she wished was very great. If I were able to see her every day, what opportunities I should have for pressing my suit! But I am glad to say that the thought of her welfare was dearer to me than my hopes even. So I conscientiously used every argument I could think of to induce her to remain where she was. But, as she listened, I saw her great eyes fill slowly with tears.

"Oh, I must go; I must go," she cried; and, burying her head in a cushion, she burst into a flood of hysterical weeping.

Her mother, hearing the commotion, flew to my assistance, but it was some time before we succeeded in quieting her. At length, she recovered sufficiently to be left to the care of her maid.

I was glad to be able to assure Mrs. Derwent that, notwithstanding the severity of the attack I had witnessed, I had detected in her daughter no symptom of insanity.

As there was no further excuse for remaining, I allowed Miss Alice to drive me away. Young Norman, who was returning to the Cowper's to fetch his bag, went with us; and his company did not add to my pleasure, I confess. I kept glancing at him, surreptitiously, anxious to discover what it was that May saw in him. He appeared to me to be a very ordinary young man. I had never, to my knowledge, met him before; yet, the longer I looked at him the more I became convinced that this was not the first time I had seen him, and, not only that, but I felt that I had some strange association with him. But what? My memory refused to give up its secret. All that night I puzzled over it, but the following morning found me with that riddle still unsolved.

CHAPTER XIII

MR. AND MRS. ATKINS AT HOME

A N urgent case necessitated my leaving Beverley at such an early hour that the city was still half asleep when I reached it. After driving from florist to florist in search of an early riser amongst them, I at last found one. I selected the choicest of his flowers, and ordered them to be sent to Miss Derwent by special messenger, hoping they would arrive in time to greet her on her awakening, and cheerfully paid the price demanded for them.

On reaching my office I was surprised to find a note from the irrepressible Atkins. You may remember, patient reader, that I had promised to dine with him on the previous evening. When I found that it would be impossible for me to do so, I sent word that I regretted that I could not keep my engagement with him. I naturally thought that that ended the matter. Not at all! Here was an invitation even more urgent than the last—an invitation for that very day, too. Unless I wished to be positively rude and to hurt the feelings of these good people, I must accept. There was no way out of it. So I scribbled a few lines to that effect.

I confess that when I rang the Atkins's bell that evening I did so with considerable trepidation, for I was not at all sure how the lady would receive me. You see I had not forgotten the way she flounced out of the room the last and only time I had seen her. And yet I had been quite blameless on that occasion. It was the Coroner's questions which had annoyed her, not mine. However, I was considerably reassured as to my reception by receiving a smiling welcome from the same pretty maid I had seen the week before. It is a queer fact that we unconsciously measure the amount of regard people have for us by the manners of their servants. That this theory is quite fallacious, I know; but I found it very useful on this occasion, for it gave me the necessary courage to enter the drawing-room with smiling composure.

The room was almost dark, and, coming from the brilliantly-lighted hall, it was some seconds before I could distinguish from its surroundings the small figure of my hostess, silhouetted against the crimson sky. Her shimmering black gown and fluffy hair caught and reflected her red background in such a way that for a moment I fancied I saw her surrounded and bespattered with blood. The effect was so uncanny that it quite startled me, but as she moved forward the illusion vanished, and I was soon shaking a soft, warm hand, which was quite reassuring.

"I just hope you don't mind the dark," she exclaimed, leading me to a chair and sinking into one herself, "but somehow the light has hurt my eyes lately, and so I don't turn it on till it is so dark that I tumble all over the furniture. Mr. Atkins says I'm crazy and ought to buy a pair of blue goggles, and so I would, only they're so unbecoming."

"On the contrary," I assured her, as I let myself cautiously down into one of those uncomfortable gilt abominations known to the trade as a Louis XVI. armchair, "I think this dim light just the thing for a chat; I always become quite confidential if I am caught between daylight and dark. The day reveals too much; it offers no veil for one's blushes. The darkness, on the other hand, having no visible limits, robs one of that sense of seclusion which alone provokes confidences. But the twilight, the tactful twilight, is so discreet that it lures one on to open one's heart. Luckily, no designing person has yet found out how weak I am at this hour, or else I should have no secrets left."

"Oh, go along," she giggled; "I guess you're not the kind to say more than you mean to."

"I assure you I am——" but here I was interrupted by my host, who called out from the threshold:

"Hello, sitting in the dark? This is really too absurd, Lulu."

A flood of light followed these words and revealed young Atkins's stalwart figure, irreproachably clad in evening dress.

"Well, I *am* glad to see you, Doctor," he cried, as he wrung my hand vigorously. "Dinner's ready, too, and I hope you're ready for it."

The folding doors leading into the next room slid back and disclosed a prettily appointed table, profusely decorated with flowers and silver. Soon after we had settled into our chairs, I seized a moment when I was unobserved to steal a look at Mrs. Atkins. She was certainly paler and thinner than when I had seen her last, but the change instead of detracting from her looks only added to her charm. Dark violet lines encircled her blue eyes and lent them a wistful, pathetic expression that greatly enhanced their beauty. Otherwise, I thought her less changed than her husband had led me to suspect and I could detect none of that extreme nervousness of which he had spoken; only when she turned towards him did her manner appear at all strained, and even this was so slight as to be hardly noticeable. In fact, of the two, it was he who seemed ill at ease, and I noticed that he kept watching her anxiously. I saw that she was conscious of his constant scrutiny and that at times she became quite restless under his prolonged gaze; then, tossing her head defiantly, as if determined to cast off the spell of his eyes, she would talk and laugh with renewed animation.

The dinner was delicious and well served; my hostess extremely pretty; my host almost overpoweringly cordial, and the conversation agreeable, if not highly intellectual. We had reached the fruit stage, and I was leaning contentedly back in my chair, congratulating myself on my good luck in having happened on such a pleasant evening, when Mrs. Atkins exclaimed:

"I say, Doctor, you haven't told us a thing about your thrilling adventure. What a blessing the madman didn't succeed in killing you. Do tell us all about it."

After her husband's warning me that the bare mention of the tragedy excited her I had naturally taken great pains to avoid all reference to the subject. I was, consequently, a good deal surprised to hear her broach it with such apparent calmness.

I glanced inquiringly at Atkins.

"Yes, do," he urged, still looking at his wife.

"I'm afraid there isn't much more to tell," I hesitatingly replied; "I gave the newspapers a pretty straight account of the whole affair."

"Oh, but you were much too modest," she cried; "a little bird has told us that you are a great detective, and suspected Argot from the first. Say, how did you manage to hit on him? We want all the details, you know."

It was her flattery, I am afraid, which loosened my tongue and made me forget my former caution.

"Well, it was mostly luck," I assured her, and then proceeded to give a long account of the whole affair.

"And now," I said, warming to my topic under their evident interest, "I wonder if either of you, when you read over the description of the murdered man, or when you saw him, for the matter of that, noticed anything peculiar about him? I confess that it escaped me and my attention had to be called to it by Mr. Merritt."

"Something peculiar," she repeated. "What kind of a peculiarity do you mean?"

"Well, the lack of an important article of apparel," I replied.

"No; I didn't notice anything out of the way," she answered, after considering the question for some minutes.

I turned towards her husband. He was leaning forward, so deeply absorbed in watching his wife as to be entirely unconscious of my presence, and on his ingenious countenance I was shocked to observe suspicion and love struggling for mastery. Struck by his silence, she, too, looked at him, and as her eyes encountered his I saw a look of fear creep into them, and the faint color fade from her cheeks. When he saw how his behaviour had affected her, he tried to pull himself together, and passed his hand swiftly over his face as if anxious to obliterate whatever might be written there.

"Well, what is this missing link?" he asked, with obviously enforced gaiety. He looked squarely at me, and, as he did so, I became convinced that he already knew the answer to that question. For a moment we stared at each other in silence. Were my looks tell-tale, I wondered, and could he see that I had discovered his secret?

"Say," broke in Mrs. Atkins, "don't go to sleep. What was this missing thing?"

I would have given anything not to have had to answer.

"No hat was found with the body," I said. Atkins, I noticed, was again looking fixedly at his wife, who had grown deathly white, and sat staring at him, as if hypnotised. Both had, apparently, forgotten me, but yet I felt deeply embarrassed at being present, and dropped my eyes to my plate so as to give them a chance to regain their composure unobserved.

"Has the hat been found?" I heard her inquire, and her high soprano voice had again that peculiar grating quality I had noticed during her interview with the Coroner.

"Yes," I answered, "it was found in Argot's possession. He actually wore it, and laid it down under my nose. Insanity can go no further."

"But how did you know it was the missing hat?" demanded Atkins, without taking his eyes off his wife.

What could I answer? I was appalled at the dilemma into which my vanity and stupidity had led me.

"I suspected it was the hat which was wanted," I blundered on, "because Mr. Merritt had told me he was looking for an ordinary white straw containing the name of a Chicago hatter. Argot's hat answered to this description, and, as the Frenchman had never been West, I concluded that he had not got it by fair means."

"So the dead man hailed from Chicago, did he?" inquired Atkins.

"The detective thinks so," I answered.

"Have the police discovered his name yet?"

"I—I am not sure!"

"You are discreet, I see."

"Indeed, no," I assured him. "The last time I saw Mr. Merritt he was still in doubt as to the man's real name."

"He only knew that the initials were A. B.," said Atkins, quickly.

I glanced, rapidly, from the husband to the wife. They sat, facing each other, unflinchingly, like two antagonists of mettle, their faces drawn and set. But the strain proved too much for the woman, and, in another moment, she would have fallen to the floor if I had not managed to catch her. Instead of assisting me, her husband sat quite still, wiping great beads of perspiration from his forehead.

"Come here," I said, "and help me to carry your wife to the window."

He got up, as if dazed, and came slowly toward me, and, together, we carried her to a lounge in the drawing-room.

"Look here, you told me yourself that all mention of the murder made your wife extremely nervous, and yet you distinctly encouraged us to talk about it this evening. Do you think that right?"

He stared at me with unseeing eyes, and appeared not to understand what I was saying.

"I had to find out the truth," he muttered.

"Look here, man," I cried, shaking him by the arm, "pull yourself together. Don't let your wife see that expression on your face when she comes to. This is not a simple faint; your wife's heart is affected, and if you excite her still further you may kill her."

That roused him, and he now joined to the best of his ability in my endeavors to restore her. She soon opened her eyes, and glanced timidly at her husband. He managed to smile affectionately at her, which seemed to reassure her.

"How stupid of me to faint!" she exclaimed, "but it was so very hot."

"Yes, the heat is dreadful; you really should not overtax yourself during this weather," said her husband, gently, laying his hand on hers. She beamed at him, while a lovely pink overspread her pale face.

"As a doctor, may I urge Mrs. Atkins to go to bed immediately?" I said.

"Oh, no, no," she cried petulantly; "I'm all right." But as she tried to stand up she staggered helplessly.

"I insist on your going to bed, Lulu; I shall carry you up-stairs at once."

And the big man picked her up without more ado. She smiled at me over his shoulder, dimpling like a pleased child.

"You see, Doctor, what a tyrant he is," she cried, waving her small hand as she disappeared.

When Atkins returned, I rose to say good night, but he motioned me to return to my seat, and handing me a box of cigars, insisted on my taking one. Then, dragging a chair forward, he sat down facing me. We puffed away for several minutes, in silence. I was sure, from his manner, that he was trying to get up his courage to tell me something.

"You said just now that Mrs. Atkins has something the matter with her heart?"

"I'm afraid so; but I do not fancy it is anything very serious, and if it is taken in time, and she leads a quiet, happy life, there is no reason that she should not recover completely."

He got up and paced the room.

"I love her," he murmured.

I watched him with increasing perplexity.

"Well, if that is so, treat her differently. You sit and watch her in a way that is enough to make anyone nervous, let alone a delicate woman. Forgive my speaking so plainly, but I consider it my duty as a physician. I am convinced that the extreme nervousness you spoke of (and which, by the way, I have failed to observe) is not to be attributed to the murder at all, but to your behaviour. I don't think you have any idea how strange that is."

"Oh, but my wife has not been nervous since the Frenchman was arrested. We watched him being taken away from your house, and last night she slept quietly for the first time since the tragedy." He paused and looked at me as if he longed to say more.

"Well, that is quite natural, I think. I can imagine nothing more alarming than to know that you are living under the same roof with an undetected criminal, who might at any time make use of his freedom to commit another murder. Till she knew who was guilty, she must have suspected and feared everybody. Now that she knows the fellow to be under lock and key, she can again sleep in peace."

Atkins sat down.

"Doctor, men of your calling are the same as confessors, are they not?"

"If you mean as regards the sanctity of professional communications, yes."

"Then I should like to confide a few things to you under the seal of that professional secrecy."

"All right; go ahead."

"Do you know that my wife is from Chicago?"

"Yes."

"I have never been there myself, and consequently know none of her friends. You may have heard that my father was very much opposed to my marriage. He collected a lot of cock-and-bull stories about my wife, which, needless to say, I did not believe. So the wedding took place, and, until a week ago, I can truthfully say that I have been perfectly happy."

"What happened then?"

"I had to go out of town for two days on business, and got back very late on Wednesday night, having been delayed by an accident on the line. I was careful to be very quiet as I let myself in, anxious not to wake up my wife, who, I expected, would be fast asleep at that hour. I was therefore surprised and pleased to find the hall still ablaze with light. So, she had sat up for me after all, I thought. Taking off my hat I turned to hang it on the rack when I noticed a strange hat among my own. I took it down and examined it. It contained the name of a Chicago hatter and the initials A. B. were stamped on the inside band. At first I was simply puzzled, then it occurred to me that its owner must be still on the premises. That thought roused all my latent jealousy, so, putting the hat quietly back, I stole on tiptoe to the parlor. Peeping through the portières, I saw my wife lying asleep on the sofa. She was quite alone. To whom then did the hat belong? What man had left in such hurry or agitation as to forget so essential a thing? All the stories my father had told me came back to me with an overwhelming rush. Then I blushed at my want of confidence. All I had to do, I assured myself, was to wake up my wife and she would explain everything at once. I should not need to ask a question even; she would of her own accord tell me about her visitor. Full of these hopes I entered the room. She opened her eyes almost immediately and greeted me with even greater warmth than usual. I responded as best I could, but my impatience to hear what she had to say was so great as to render me insensible to everything else. I soon led our talk round to what she had been doing during my absence. She told me in a general way, but, Doctor, she made no mention of a gentleman visitor! I think I was patient. Again and again I gave her the chance to confide in me. At last, I asked her right out if she had happened to see any of her Chicago friends. She hesitated a minute, then answered, deliberately, No! To doubt was no longer possible. She was concealing something from me; therefore, there was something to conceal.

And yet she dared to hang around my neck and nestle close to me. It made me sick to feel the false creature so near. I don't know what came over me. The room swam before my eyes, and starting to my feet I flung her from me. She fell in a heap by the window and lay quite still, staring at me with speechless terror. I had had no intention of hurting her and was horrified at my brutality. I went to her and tried to raise her up, but at my approach she shrieked aloud and shrank away from me. I was thoroughly ashamed now and begged her to forgive my behaviour. But for some time she only shook her head, till at last, overcome by her emotions, she burst into hysterical sobs. This was too much for me. I forgot everything except that I loved her, and, kneeling down, gathered her into my arms. She no longer resisted me, but like a tired child let me do with her what I would. I carried her upstairs and soon had the satisfaction of seeing her fall asleep. From that day to this neither of us has ever referred to this occurrence! I didn't, because—well, my motives were very mixed. In the first place, I couldn't apologize for my behaviour without telling her the reason first, and that I was unwilling to do unasked. I was ashamed of my suspicions, and wanted the explanation to be offered by her and not solicited by me. And then, underlying everything, was an unacknowledged dread of what I might discover, and terror that I might again forget myself. But what were her reasons for never asking for the meaning of my conduct? Why did she not make me sue on my knees for pardon? She has always made a great fuss whenever I have offended her before; why did she pass over this outrage in silence? Did she fear what questions I might ask? Did she suspect the cause of my anger? That night, before going to bed, I took that accursed hat and flung it out of the dining-room window. It fell to the court below, and there Argot must have picked it up."

"When did you first become convinced that that hat had belonged to the murdered man?"

"Not for several days. In fact, I have never been perfectly sure till this evening."

"Really?"

"Yes; you see it did not occur to me for some time that there was any connection between my wife's visitor and the—the victim." Here the poor fellow shuddered. "Her manner was slightly constrained, and I saw she was depressed, but I thought that a natural result of the coolness that had arisen between us. I soon found out, however, that although our strained relations might weigh on her somewhat, the chief cause of her trouble was the murder. She hardly ever spoke of it, but I could see that it was never out of her mind. She used to send out for all the papers and pore over them by the hour, and was so nervous that it was positively painful to be in the room with her. She would start and scream with or without provocation. Another peculiarity she developed was an extreme disinclination to leaving the house. She went out on Thursday afternoon, I believe, but from that day to the time of Argot's arrest I don't think she ever left the building unless I insisted on it. And another queer thing she did, was to stand behind the curtains and peer at your house. I would catch her doing this at all hours of the day and night. Then I began to wonder more and more why this murder had such an effect on her. I read and re-read all that was printed about it, and suddenly it came to me that no hat had been found with the body. I searched the papers again feverishly. I had not been mistaken. Every article of clothing was carefully enumerated, but no hat was mentioned. It was then I first suspected that the dead man and my wife's visitor were one and the same person. It was an awful moment, Doctor."

He paused a while to control his emotions. "After that I kept continually puzzling as to how the fellow could have come by his death. Thank God, I was quite sure my little wife had no hand in that! You say Argot killed him; perhaps he did, though I can't imagine why or how. As soon as Mrs. Atkins heard that the Frenchman had been arrested her whole manner changed. Her nervousness disappeared as if by magic, and to-day she resumed her usual mode of life. She has even talked about the murder occasionally. But the barrier between us has not diminished. I can not forget that she concealed that man's visit from me. I have longed, yet dreaded, to have the police discover his identity, fearing that if they did his connection with my wife would also come out; and yet so anxious am I to know the nature of that connection as to be willing to run almost any risk to discover the truth. But things have come to a crisis to-night. We can no longer go on living side by side with this secret between us. She must tell me what there was between them. And now, when I can bear the suspense no longer, you insist that she must not be excited."

I felt terribly sorry for the poor fellow, and hesitated what to advise.

"Get a good doctor," I said at last, "and have Mrs. Atkins's heart examined. Her trouble may not be as serious as I think it is, and in that case there would be no further need of caution."

"Won't you undertake the case?"

"Have you no family physician?"

"Yes; Dr. Hartley."

"He is an excellent man, and I think it would be much less agitating to Mrs. Atkins to be treated by her own doctor. You see it is very important that she should be kept quiet. I should like to ask you one thing, however: Don't you think you ought to tell the police that it was you who first found the hat and who threw it into the yard?"

"I don't think it the least necessary," he answered, in great alarm; "what harm can this additional suspicion do Argot? There is no doubt that he tried to murder you, and is quite irresponsible. Why should he not be guilty of the other crime? You suspected him before you knew that the hat was in his possession."

"That is all very true. And the man is hopelessly insane, I hear, and, guilty or not guilty, will probably spend the rest of his life in a lunatic asylum. Well, I must be off. Let me know what Dr. Hartley's verdict is. I am especially anxious that my fears may prove groundless, because I am sure that if you and Mrs. Atkins could have a frank talk everything would soon be satisfactorily explained."

"Do you think so?" he exclaimed, eagerly.

"I'm sure of it," and, with a hearty handshake, I left him.

HAPTER XIV

T HAT night I could not sleep, and when on receiving my mail the next morning I found that it contained no line from Fred, my anxiety could no longer be kept within bounds, and I determined that, come what might, another day should not pass without my seeing May Derwent. I left the hospital as soon as I decently could, but, even so, it was almost one o'clock before I was once more on my way to Beverley. On arriving there, I found to my disgust that there were no cabs at the station. An obliging countryman offered to "hitch up a team," but I declined, thinking it would be quicker to walk than to wait for it, as the Derwents' house was hardly a mile off. A delicious breeze had sprung up and was blowing new life into me, and I should have enjoyed my walk except for the fact that, as my visit must necessarily be a very short one, I begrudged every minute spent away from May Derwent. I was, therefore, trudging along at a great rate, entirely absorbed in reaching my destination in the shortest possible time, when I was surprised to perceive in the distance a woman running rapidly towards me. As there was neither man nor beast in sight, I wondered at the reason of her haste. A sudden illness? A fire? As the flying figure drew nearer, I was dismayed to recognize May Derwent. I rushed forward to meet her, and a moment later she lay panting and trembling in my arms. As I looked down and saw her fair head lying on my breast I felt as if I were having a foretaste of heaven. I was recalled to earth by feeling her slight form shudder convulsively and by hearing an occasional frightened sob.

"What has happened, May? What has frightened you?" I feared that she would resent this use of her Christian name, but she evidently did not notice it, for she only clung the tighter to me.

Mrs. Derwent, whose approach I had been watching, here joined us, hot and out of breath from her unwonted exertion. Her indignation at finding May in the arms of a comparative stranger was such that she dragged her daughter quite roughly from me.

"You must really calm yourself, May," she commanded, with more severity than I had thought her capable of.

But the poor child only continued to tremble and cry. As it seemed a hopeless undertaking to try and quiet her, Mrs. Derwent and I each took her by an arm and between us we assisted her home. As we were nearing it, I saw

Norman hurrying towards us.

"What's the matter?" he inquired, anxiously.

As May had grown gradually more composed, her mother felt she could now leave her to my care, and, joining Norman, they walked briskly ahead, an arrangement which I don't think that young man at all relished.

My darling and I strolled slowly on, she leaning confidingly on me, and I was well content.

"You are not frightened, now?" I asked.

She raised her beautiful eyes for an instant to mine.

"No," she murmured; and all I could see of her averted face was one small crimson ear.

"I hope you will never be afraid when I am with you," I said, pressing her arm gently to my side. She did not withdraw from me, only hung her head lower, so I went on bravely.

"These last forty-four hours have been the longest and most intolerable of my life!"

She elevated her eyebrows, and I thought I perceived a faint smile hovering around her lips.

"Indeed!"

"I hope you got some flowers I sent you yesterday?"

"Yes. Didn't you receive my note thanking you for them? They were very beautiful!"

I loudly anathematised the post which had delayed so important a message.

This time there was no doubt about it—and a roguish smile was parting her lips. This emboldened me to ask: "Were these roses as good as the first lot? I got them at a different place."

"Oh, did you send those also? There was no card with them."

"I purposely omitted to enclose one, as I feared you might consider that I was presuming on our slight acquaintance. Besides, I doubted whether you would remember me or had even caught my name."

"I had not."

There was a pause.

"Oh, what must you have thought of me! What must you think of me!" she exclaimed, in tones of deep distress, trying to draw her arm away. But I held her fast.

"Believe me, I entertain for you the greatest respect and admiration. I should never dream of criticising anything you do or might have done."

She shot a grateful glance at me, and seeing we were unobserved I ventured to raise her small gloved hand reverently to my lips. She blushed again, but did not repulse me.

On arriving at the house, I insisted on her lying down, and, hoping the quiet would do her good, we left her alone. On leaving the room, we passed Norman pacing up and down outside, like a faithful dog. He did not offer to join us, but remained at his post.

I had not questioned May as to the cause of her fright, fearing to excite her, but I was none the less anxious to know what had occurred. Luckily, Mrs. Derwent was as eager to enlighten me as I was to learn.

"You know, Doctor Fortescue, how I have tried lately to keep everything away from my daughter which could possibly agitate her. However, when she suggested that she would like to walk to the village I gladly acquiesced, never dreaming that on a quiet country road anything could occur to frighten her, nervous as she was. With the exception of last Sunday, this was the first time since her return from New York that she had been willing to go outside the gate; therefore I was especially glad she should have this little change. I offered to accompany her or rather them (for Mr. Norman, of course, joined us), and we all three started off together. When we had gone some distance from the house, Mr. Norman remembered an important letter which he had left on his writing-table and which he was most anxious should catch the mid-day mail. So he turned back to get it. I noticed at the time that May appeared very reluctant to have him go. I even thought that she was on the point of asking him not to leave her, but I was glad to see that she controlled herself, for her horror of being separated from that young man has seemed to me not only silly, but very compromising. So we walked on alone, but very slowly, so that he could easily overtake us. The road was pretty, the day heavenly, and my shaken spirits were lighter than they had been for some time." Mrs. Derwent paused a moment to wipe her eyes. "Did you happen to notice," she continued, "that clump of bushes near the bend of the road?"

"Certainly."

"Well, just as we were passing those I caught sight of a horrid-looking tramp, lying on his back, half hidden by the undergrowth. May was sauntering along swinging her parasol, which she had not opened, as our whole way had lain in the shade. She evidently did not see the fellow, but I watched him get up and follow us on the other side of the bushes. I was a little frightened, but before I could decide what I had better do he had approached May and said something to her which I was unable to catch. It must have been something very dreadful, for she uttered a piercing shriek, and turning on him like a young tigress hit him several times violently over the head with her sunshade. Dropping everything, she fled from the scene. You know the rest."

The last words were spoken a trifle austerely, and I saw that Mrs. Derwent had not forgotten the position in which she had found her daughter, although she probably considered that that position was entirely due to May's hysterical condition and that I had been an innocent factor in the situation.

"What became of the tramp?" I inquired, eagerly. "I saw no one following your daughter."

"He did not do so. I stood for a moment watching her tear down the road, and when again I remembered the man I found he had disappeared."

"Would you know the fellow, if you saw him again?"

"Certainly! He was an unusually repulsive specimen of his tribe."

As Mrs. Derwent had failed to recognise him, the man could not have been her son, as I had for a moment feared.

"By the way, Doctor, May is still bent on going to New York."

"Well, perhaps it is advisable that she should do so."

"But why?"

"The quiet of the country does not seem to be doing her much good, does it? Let us, therefore, try the excitement of New York, and see what effect that will have. Besides, I am very anxious to have Miss Derwent see some great nerve specialist. I am still a very young practitioner, and I confess her case baffles me."

"I see that you fear that she is insane!" cried Mrs. Derwent.

"Indeed, I do not," I assured her, "but I think her nerves are very seriously out of order. If she goes on like this, she will soon be in a bad way. If you wish me to do so, I will find out what specialist I can most easily get hold of, and make arrangements for his seeing your daughter with as little delay as possible."

"Thank you."

My time was now almost up, so I asked to see my patient again, so as to assure myself that she was none the worse for her fright.

I found her with her eyes open, staring blankly at the ceiling, and, from time to time, her body would still twitch convulsively. However, she welcomed us with a smile, and her pulse was decidedly stronger. It was a terrible trial to me to see that lovely girl lying there, and to feel that, so far, I had been powerless to help her. I thought that, perhaps, if she talked of her recent adventure it would prevent her brooding over it. So, after sympathising with her in a general way, I asked what the tramp had said to terrify her so much. She shook her head feebly.

"I could not make out what he was saying."

I glanced upwards, and caught a look of horror on her mother's face.

"Oh, indeed," I said; "it was just his sudden appearance which frightened you so much?"

"Yes," she answered, wearily. "Oh, I wish I could go to New York," she sighed.

"I have just persuaded your mother to spend a few days there."

She glanced quickly from one to the other.

"Really?"

Mrs. Derwent nodded a tearful assent.

"And when are we going?" she demanded.

"To-morrow, if you are well enough."

"Oh! thank you."

"But what will you do with your guest?"

"Mr. Norman? Oh, he will come, too;" but she had the grace to look apologetic.

Once outside the room, Mrs. Derwent beckoned me into her *boudoir*.

"Well, Doctor Fortescue," she exclaimed, "what do you think of that? May turns on a harmless beggar, who has done nothing to annoy her, and beats him! She is not at all ashamed of her behaviour, either."

"I confess, Mrs. Derwent, I am surprised."

"Oh, she must be crazy," wailed the poor lady.

"No, madam—simply hysterical—I am sure of it. Still, this makes me more than ever wishful to have another opinion about her case."

Before we parted, it had been decided that the choice of suitable rooms should be left to me.

Back again in New York, I went immediately in search of them. I was so difficult to satisfy that it was some time before I selected a suite overlooking the Park, which seemed to me to answer all demands.

May and her mother were not expected till the following afternoon, so I tried to kill the intervening time by making the place look homelike, and I succeeded, I think. Masses of flowers and palms filled every nook, and the newest magazines and books lay on the tables.

I met the ladies at the station, where they parted from Norman, whom I had begun to regard as inevitable. It was, therefore, with a feeling of exultation that I drove alone with them to their hotel.

When May saw the bower I had prepared for her she seemed really pleased, and thanked me very prettily.

I left them, after a few minutes, but not until they had promised to dine with me at a restaurant that evening.

CHAPTER XV

A SUDDEN FLIGHT

O NE of the many things and people which I am sorry to say my new occupation as Squire of Dames had caused me to neglect, was poor Madame Argot. On leaving the Derwents, I determined to call on her at once. To my surprise, I found Mrs. Atkins there before me. The poor Frenchwoman was crying bitterly.

"Look here!" I said, after we had exchanged greetings; "this will never do. My patient must not be allowed to excite herself in this way."

"Ah, mais monsieur," she cried, "what vill you? I mus' veep; zink only; vone veek ago an' I 'appy voman; now all gone. My 'usban', 'e mad, and zey zay 'e murderer too, but I zay, No, no."

Mrs. Atkins patted her hand gently.

"Monsieur Stuah, 'e tell me to go," she continued, "an' I don' know vere; me not speak English vera good, an' I mus' go alone vid peoples zat speak no French. Ah, I am a miserable, lonely woman," she sobbed.

Mrs. Atkins consoled her as best she could, and promised to get her a congenial place. It was a pretty sight to see the dashing little woman in that humble bed-room, and I had never admired her so much. When she got up to leave, I rose also, and, not wishing to pass through Mr. Stuart's apartments, we left the building by the back way. When we were in the street, Mrs. Atkins started to walk up town.

"Are you going for a walk?" I asked.

"Yes; it is much cooler to-day, and I really must get a little exercise."

"Do you mind my joining you?" I inquired.

"I'd be glad of your company," she answered, cordially.

"It's terribly sad about that poor woman, isn't it?" she said, as we sauntered along.

"It is, indeed," I replied; "and the hospital authorities give no hope of her husband's recovery."

"I suppose there is no doubt that he killed the man?"

Here we were again on this dangerous topic, and I glanced quickly at her, fearing a repetition of last night's attack.

She noticed my hesitation, and laughed.

"Oh, you needn't be so afraid of what you say. I ain't going to faint again. I want to know the truth, though, and I can't see why you shouldn't tell me."

"Well, if you insist upon it," I said, "here it is: I really don't know whether he is guilty or not; I have been convinced that he was till very recently, but Merritt (the detective, you know) has always been sceptical, and maintains that a woman committed the murder."

"A woman," she repeated, turning her eyes full on me. "But what woman?"

"Merritt refuses to tell me whom he suspects, but he promises to produce the fair criminal before next Tuesday."

We walked on for about a block, when, struck by her silence, I looked at her, and saw that she had grown alarmingly pale. I cursed myself for my loquacity, but what could I have done? It is almost impossible to avoid answering direct questions without being absolutely rude, and as I knew the detective did not suspect her I really could not see why she should be so agitated.

"I guess I'm not very strong," she said; "I'm tired already, and think I'll go home."

I wondered if my society had been disagreeable or, at any rate, inopportune, and had caused her to cut short her walk.

As we repassed my house, I caught Mrs. Atkins peering apprehensively at it. I followed the direction of her eyes, but could see nothing unusual.

When I got back to my office, I found that Atkins had called during my absence; I was very sorry to have missed him, as he no doubt came to report what Dr. Hartley had said about his wife.

That night I was called out to see a patient, and returned home during the small hours of the morning. I was still some distance from my house when I distinctly saw the back door of the Rosemere open, and a muffled figure steal out. I was too far away to be able to distinguish any details. I could not even be sure whether the figure was that of a man or a woman. I hastened my steps as I saw it cross the street, but before I had come within reasonable distance of it, it had disappeared round the corner.

The next morning I was aroused at a very early hour by a vigorous ringing at my bell. Hurrying to the door, I was astonished to find Atkins there. He was white and trembling. I pulled him into the room and made him sit down.

"What is the matter?" I asked, as I went to the sideboard and poured out a stiff glass of brandy, which I handed him. "Drink that, and you'll feel better," I said.

He gulped it down at one swallow.

"My wife has disappeared."

"Disappeared!" I repeated.

He nodded.

"But when?—how?"

"I don't know. At dinner yesterday she acted queerly. The tears kept coming to her eyes without any reason——"

"Before you go any further," I interrupted him, "tell me if this was after the doctor had seen her?"

"Yes, and he practically confirmed all you said. He laid great stress on her being spared all agitation, and advised a course of baths at Nauheim."

"Her tears, then, were probably caused by worrying over her condition," I said.

"I don't think so, for the doctor was very careful to reassure her, and I had not even mentioned that we were to go abroad. No, it was something else, I'm sure." He paused. I wondered if anything I had said during our short walk had upset her.

"I suggested going to a roof garden," continued Atkins, "and she acquiesced enthusiastically, and after that was over she insisted on a supper at Rector's. It was pretty late when we got home, and we both went immediately to bed. Now, I assure you that ever since she fainted on Wednesday I have been most affectionate towards her. I had determined to bury my suspicions, and my anxiety for her health helped me to do so. She responded very tenderly to my caresses, but I could see that she was still as depressed as before, although she tried her best to hide it from me. I tell you all this so that you may know that nothing occurred yesterday between us that could have caused her to leave me, and yet that is what she has done."

He buried his head in his arms. I laid my hand on his shoulder.

"Tell me the rest, old man."

"The rest?—I woke up a short time ago and was surprised to find my wife had already left the room. Wondering what could be the matter (for she is usually a very late riser), I got up also. On the table beside my bed lay a letter addressed to me in her handwriting. I tore it open. Here it is," and he handed me a small pink note redolent of the peculiar scent which I had noticed his wife affected. This is what I read:

My Darling Husband:

I must leave you. It is best for both. Don't think I'm going because I don't love you. It isn't that. I love you more than ever. It breaks my heart to go. Oh, my darling, darling! We have been happy, haven't we? And now it is all over. Don't look for me, I beg you. I must hide. Don't tell any one, even the servants, that I have gone, for two days. Oh, do oblige me in this. I have taken all the money I could find, $46.00, and some of my jewelry; so I shall not be destitute.

Forgive me, and forget me.

Your loving, heart-broken wife,

Lulu.

After reading the note to the end, I stared at him in speechless astonishment.

"What do you think of that?" he asked.

"Well, really, of all mysterious, incomprehensible——"

"Exactly," he interrupted, impatiently, "but what am I to do now? It is, of course, nonsense her telling me not to look for her. I *will* look for her and find her, too. But how shall I go about it? O my God, to think of that little girl sick, unhappy, alone; she will die——" he cried, starting up.

"Atkins," I said, after a moment's reflection, "I think the best thing for you to do is to lay this case before Mr. Merritt."

"What, the man who was mixed up in the murder? Never!"

"You can hardly speak of a detective as being mixed up in a murder," I said. "Every celebrated detective has always several important cases going at once, one of which is very likely to be a murder. The reason I suggest Merritt is that I have seen a good deal of him lately, and have been much impressed by his character as well as his ability. He is a kindly, honourable, and discreet man, and that is more than can be said for the majority of his fellows, and, professionally, he stands at the very top of the ladder. You want to find your wife as quickly as possible, and at the same time to avoid all publicity. You therefore must consult a thoroughly reliable as well as competent person."

"But if I go to Merritt and tell him that my wife has disappeared, I must also tell of the strange way she has been behaving lately. That will lead to his discovering that the murdered man was a friend of hers, and who knows but that he may end by suspecting her of complicity in his death?—and I acknowledge that her flight lends some colour to that theory."

"My dear fellow, he has been aware for some time—since Monday, in fact —that the dead man visited your wife the very evening he was killed, and yet, knowing all this, he told me that Mrs. Atkins could not be connected in the remotest way with the tragedy."

116

"He said that!" exclaimed Atkins, with evident relief.

"He did," I assured him.

"All right, then; let's go to him at once."

As soon as I was dressed we got into a cab and drove rapidly to Mr. Merritt's. We met the detective just going out, but he at once turned back with us, and we were soon sitting in his little office. Atkins was so overcome by the situation that I found it necessary to explain our errand. The detective, on hearing of Mrs. Atkins's flight gave a slight start.

"I wish I knew at what time she left home," he said.

"I think I can help you there,"—and I told him of the person I had seen stealing from the building, and who I now believed to have been no other than Mrs. Atkins.

"Half-past two," he murmured; "I wonder she left as early as that. Where could she have gone to at that hour! It looks as if she had arranged her flight beforehand and prepared some place of refuge. Do you know of any friend in the city she would be likely to appeal to in such an emergency?" he inquired, turning towards Atkins.

"No," he replied; "whatever friends she has here have all been previously friends of mine, and as she has only known them since our marriage they have not had time to become very intimate yet."

After asking a few more pertinent questions, Mr. Merritt rose.

"I think I have all the necessary facts now and will at once order the search started. I hope soon to have good news for you."

We all three left the detective's house together, but separated immediately afterwards. Atkins, haggard and wild-eyed, went off to look for his wife himself. I had to go to the hospital, and Merritt offered to accompany me there.

"Well, what do you think of this latest development?" I asked.

"I am not surprised."

"Not surprised!" I exclaimed; "what do you mean?"

"Just this: I have been expecting Mrs. Atkins to make an attempt to escape, and have tried to prevent her doing so."

"How?" I inquired.

"One of my men has been watching her night and day. He is stationed in your house, and I am extremely annoyed that he has allowed her to slip through his fingers, although I must say he has some excuse, for she certainly managed things very neatly."

"But Mr. Merritt," I exclaimed, "do you now think Mrs. Atkins guilty?"

He smiled enigmatically, but said nothing.

"This is a very serious matter for me," I continued. "After what you repeatedly said to me, I thought you scouted the probability of her being in any way implicated in this murder. It was on the strength of this assurance that I induced Atkins to confide in you. Had I known that you were having her shadowed I shouldn't, of course, have advised him to put his case in your hands. I feel dreadfully about this. It is exactly as if I had betrayed the poor fellow. I must warn him at once."

I stopped.

"Don't do anything rash," he urged, laying a detaining hand on my arm.

"But——"

"I quite understand your feelings," he continued, looking at me with his kindly blue eyes. "When I first heard the nature of your errand I felt a good deal embarrassed. But it was then too late. What I knew, I knew. I assure you, Doctor, that what I have heard this morning, far from assisting me to solve the Rosemere mystery, will prove a positive hindrance to my doing so. I shall no longer feel at liberty to employ ruse or strategy in my dealings with the lady, and if I find her shall have to treat her with the utmost consideration."

"Do you think she murdered the man? Is she the woman whose name you promised to reveal next Tuesday?"

"I must decline to answer that question."

I glanced at him for a minute in silence.

"If I am not mistaken, this flight will precipitate matters," he went on, reflectively. "If the right party hears of it, I expect an explosion will follow."

"Don't talk in enigmas, Mr. Merritt; either say what you mean or——" I paused.

"Hold your tongue," he concluded, with a smile. "You are quite right. And as I can't say any more at present, I will say nothing. By the way, I hear Mrs. and Miss Derwent and Mr. Norman are in town."

"Yes," I curtly assented. "Well, Mr. Merritt," I went on, abruptly changing the subject, "I must leave you now. I am very much upset by your attitude towards Mrs. Atkins. I am not yet sure that I shall not tell her husband. Together, we may perhaps prevent her falling into your hands."

The detective smiled indulgently as we parted. I saw now all the harm I had done. Poor Mrs. Atkins had feared from the first that she might be suspected, and having discovered that she was being watched, had naturally been unwilling to leave the protection of her own home. When Argot was arrested she thought all danger was over, till I stupidly blurted out that the detective was stalking a woman, not a man. Then she fled. And she chose the middle of the night, reasoning, no doubt, that at that hour the sleuth would most likely be off his guard. Since I had known her and her husband better, I could no longer suspect her, and I now tried to remember all the arguments Merritt had formerly used to prove her innocence. Foolish she might have been, but criminal, never,—I concluded. And it was I who had put her enemies on her track!

CHAPTER XVI

THAT TACTLESS DETECTIVE

H ER visit to town had certainly done May no harm. On the day of their arrival, she and her mother dined with me at the newest thing in restaurants, and we went afterwards to a roof garden. I had provided a man of an age suitable to Mrs. Derwent to make up the party, and so the evening passed pleasantly for all—delightfully for me. For, to my great relief, May seemed really better. With flushed cheeks and sparkling eyes, she flitted gaily from one topic to another, and only occasionally did she give one of her nervous starts. Her good spirits kept up nearly to the end, when she suddenly sank back into the state of apathy, which, alas! I knew so well.

Mrs. Derwent had taken care to inform me that Norman had called late that afternoon to inquire how they had borne the journey, and had been surprised to hear that they were dining out. Was this a hint that I should have invited him also? If so, it was one that I did not mean to take. Having at last succeeded in parting him from May, I was determined not to be the one to bring them together again.

I had decided, in deference to May's morbid horror of seeing a doctor, that it would be better that her first interview with the nerve specialist should take place under circumstances which would lead her to suppose that their meeting was purely accidental. Thinking herself unnoticed, she would put no restraint on herself, and he would thus be able to judge much more easily of the full extent of her peculiarities. Mrs. Derwent and I had therefore arranged that we should all lunch together on the day following their arrival in town. Atkins's affairs, however, detained me so long that I was almost late for my appointment, and when I at last got to the Waldorf, I found the doctor already waiting for me.

Luckily, the ladies were also late, so that I had ample time before they turned up to describe May's symptoms, and to give him a hurried account of what we knew of her experiences at the Rosemere. When she at last appeared, very pale, but looking lovelier than ever, in a trailing blue gown, I saw that he was much impressed by her. Her manner was languid rather than nervous, and she greeted us both with quiet dignity. Notwithstanding the object of the lunch, it passed off very pleasantly, and I am sure no one could have guessed from our behaviour that it was not a purely social occasion. Doctor Storrs especially was wonderful, and was soon chatting and laughing with May as if he had known her all her life. After lunch, Mrs. Derwent and I retired to a distant corner. The Doctor led the young lady to a window seat, and I was glad to see that they were soon talking earnestly to each other. I didn't dare to watch them, for fear she might suspect that we had arranged this interview. Doctor Storrs kept her there almost an hour, and when they at last joined us she looked quite ghastly, and her mouth quivered pathetically.

As we stood in the hall, waiting for the ladies' sunshades to be brought, I was astonished and annoyed to see Merritt coming towards us. He caught Miss Derwent's eye and bowed. She smiled and bowed in return, which encouraged him to join us.

"How do you do? I trust you are well," he stammered. He seemed quite painfully embarrassed, which surprised me, as I should never have thought him capable of shyness.

"Quite well, thank you," she answered, graciously, evidently pitying his confusion.

"That was a dreadful affair at the Rosemere," he bungled on, twisting his hat nervously round and round.

She drew herself up.

"I suppose the Doctor has told you the latest development of that affair?" he plunged on, regardless of her stiffness.

I stared at him in surprise; what was the matter with the man?

"No," she answered, looking anxiously at me.

"Well, he's discreet; you see we don't want it to get into the papers—" he paused, as if waiting to be questioned.

"What has happened?" struggled through her ashen lips.

"I don't know if you know Mrs. Atkins," he went on, more glibly; "she's a young bride, who has an apartment at the Rosemere."

She shook her head impatiently.

"Well, this lady has disappeared," he went on, lowering his voice; "and we very much fear that she has fled because she knew more about that murder than she should have done."

Miss Derwent tottered, and steadied herself against a table, but Mr. Merritt, with surprising denseness, failed to notice her agitation, and continued:

"It's very sad for her husband. Such a fine young fellow, and only married since May! He has been driven almost crazy by her flight. Of course, it's difficult to pity a murderess, and yet, when I think of that poor young thing forced to fly from her home in the middle of the night, I can't help feeling sorry for her. Luckily, she has heart disease, so that the agitation of being hunted from one place to another will probably soon kill her. That would be the happiest solution for all concerned."

The sunshades having been brought, Mrs. Derwent, after glancing several times impatiently at her daughter, at last moved towards her, but the latter motioned her back.

"Excuse me, Mamma, but I must say a few more words to this gentleman. I should like to know some more about Mrs. Atkins," she continued, turning again to the detective. "What made her think she was suspected?"

"Well, you see, the dead man was a friend of hers, and had been calling on her the very evening he was murdered. The fellow's name was Allan Brown, and we have discovered that a good many years ago he was credited with being one of her admirers. I guess that's true, too; but he was a worthless chap, and she no doubt turned him down. At all events, he disappeared from Chicago, and we doubt if she has seen him since. Our theory is, that when he found out that she was rich, and married, he tried to blackmail her. We know that he was drunk at the time of his death, and so we think that, in a fit of desperation, she killed him. It was a dreadful thing to do. I don't say it wasn't, but if you had seen her—so small, so ill, so worn by anxiety and remorse—I don't think you could help wishing she might escape paying the full penalty of her crime."

"I do hope so. What is her name, did you say?"

"Mrs. Lawrence P. Atkins."

"Mrs. Lawrence P. Atkins," she repeated. "And you cannot find her?"

"We have not yet been able to do so."

"This is too dreadful; how I pity the poor husband." And her eyes sought her mother, and rested on her with an expression I could not fathom.

The detective stood watching the girl for a moment, then, with a low bow, finally took himself off. My parting nod was very curt. Could any one have been more awkward, more tactless, more indiscreet, than he had been during his conversation with Miss Derwent? Was the man drunk? And what did he mean by talking about the Atkins's affairs in this way?

As the girl turned to say good-bye I was struck by a subtle change that had come over her; a great calm seemed to have settled upon her and a strange, steady light burnt in her eyes.

As I was anxious to have a private talk with the Doctor, I jumped into an automobile with him, for he had only just enough time to catch his train.

"Well, Doctor Storrs, what do you think of the young lady's case?"

"That girl is no more insane than I am, Fortescue. She is suffering from some terrible shock, but even now she has more self-control than nine women out of ten. What kind of a shock she has had I don't know, but am sure it is connected in some way with the Rosemere murder. If you ever do discover its exact nature, mark my words, you will find she has been through some ghastly experience and has borne up with amazing fortitude."

"What do you think ought to be done for her?"

"You will find that there is very little that can be done. Something is still hanging over her, I am sure; in fact she hinted as much to me. Now, unless we can find out the cause of her trouble and remove it, it is useless to look for an amelioration of her condition. In the meantime, let her have her head. She knows what she has to struggle against; we don't."

"It's all very mysterious, but I wish we could help her."

We had now reached his destination, and, with a hurried farewell, he disappeared into the station.

I had promised Mrs. Derwent to let her know immediately the result of my talk with Storrs, so, without alighting, I drove at once to the hotel. In order to avoid arousing May's suspicions by calling so soon again, Mrs. Derwent had agreed to meet me in the hotel parlour. I told her as briefly as I could what the Doctor had said. When I had finished, I saw that she was struggling with conflicting emotions.

"What can have happened to her? Oh, it is all so dreadful that I don't know what to think or fear."

"Can't you get your daughter to confide in you?"

"I will try," she murmured, as the large tears stole down her white cheeks, and, rising, she held out her long slender hand, on which sparkled a few handsome rings. As she stood there—tall, stately, still beautiful, in spite of her sufferings, her small, classic head crowned with a wreath of silvery hair—she looked like some afflicted queen, and I pitied her from the bottom of my heart. But was not my distress as great as hers!

On leaving the poor lady I hurried back to my office, where I found Atkins sitting in a miserable heap. He looked so dreadfully ill that I was alarmed.

"Have you had anything to eat to-day?" I asked. He shook his head in disgust. Without another word, I rang for my boy, and in a quarter of an hour a very passable little meal was spread on my table.

"Now, eat that," I said. He frowned, and shook his head.

"Atkins, you are behaving like a child; you must not fall ill now, or what will become of your wife?"

He hesitated a minute, then sat obediently down. I drew up a chair also, and, by playing with some fruit, pretended to be sharing his meal. The more I watched him the more I became convinced that something must be done to relieve the tension under which he suffered. A new emotion might serve the purpose; so I said:

"I have just found out some interesting facts about the murdered man."

He dropped his knife and fork.

"What?" he gasped.

"Nothing at all derogatory to your wife, I assure you; I am more than ever convinced that a frank talk would have cleared up your little misunderstanding long ago."

"Really?"

"Yes, and I'll tell you the whole story, only you must eat."

He fell to with feverish haste, his hollow eyes fixed on my face.

"Your wife's visitor was not a friend of hers, and Merritt (here I strained a point) is sure she has not met him for years. He used to be one of her admirers till she refused to see him, and then he left Chicago and has not been seen there since; but he has a bad record in several other cities. The night he was killed he came to your apartment drunk, and the detective thinks he probably tried to get money from your wife. It seems to me natural that she should have concealed his visit. He was not a guest to be proud of, and, besides, she may have been afraid of rousing your jealousy, for you are pretty jealous, you know."

"What a crazy fool I have been; I deserve to lose her. But," he inquired, with renewed suspicion, "why has she run away?"

"Because she found out that the fact that the dead man had gone to the Rosemere to see her had become known to the police, for when I saw her yesterday afternoon I blurted out that the detective did not believe in Argot's guilt, but was on the track of some female. She at once jumped to the conclusion that he suspected her, and decided to fly before she could be apprehended, and so save her life and your honour."

"Well, Doctor," he cried, pushing his plate away, "I feel better. Your news is such a relief. I must now be off again. I can't rest. Oh, how I wish I might be the one to find my little girl!"

"I do hope you will; only don't be disappointed if you are not immediately successful; New York is a big place, remember. But till you do find your wife I wish that instead of going back to your apartment you would stay here with me; we are both alone, and would be company for each other."

"Thank you; if I don't find her, I'll accept your offer. You're awfully kind, Doctor."

The poor fellow turned up again, footsore and weary, at about twelve that night. He was too exhausted by that time to suffer much, but I gave him a sedative so as to make sure of his having a good sleep.

CHAPTER XVII

ONE WOMAN EXONERATED

A TKINS and I were still at breakfast when, to my surprise, the detective was announced.

Atkins started to his feet.

"Any news of my wife?" he inquired, anxiously.

"None, I regret to say," answered Merritt.

I was still very much annoyed with him for having been so indiscreet and tactless in his interview with May Derwent, but he looked so dejected that my anger melted a little.

Atkins left us almost immediately, and started on his weary search. When he was gone, I motioned Merritt to take his place.

"Have you had any breakfast?"

"Well, not much, I confess. I was in such a hurry to hear whether anything had been heard of Mrs. Atkins or not that I only gulped down a cup of coffee before coming here."

"You must have something at once," I urged. "Here's some beefsteak and I'll ring for the boy to——"

"Hold on a moment. Are you very sure the hatchet is buried?" he inquired, with a quizzical smile.

"For the time being, certainly," I laughed. "But I reserve the right of digging it up again unless things turn out as I wish them to."

A sad look came over his face.

"Ah, Doctor, things so rarely do turn out just as one wishes them to!"

"And now, Merritt," I demanded, when, breakfast being over, we had lighted our cigars, "will you kindly tell me what made you talk as you did yesterday to Miss Derwent?"

"I had a purpose."

"What possible good could it do to remind Miss Derwent of an incident which all her friends are most anxious to have her forget?"

"It may do no good."

"Do you think you have the right to harrow a delicate girl unnecessarily?"

"Have a little patience, Doctor; I am not a brute!"

"And to talk of Mrs. Atkins as you did! Don't you know that her husband especially wishes to keep her flight secret?"

"I know. But Miss Derwent is no gossip."

"How do you know?"

"Hold on, Doctor; I'm not in the witness box yet. Can't you wait a day or two?"

A commotion in the hall put an end to our conversation. Merritt and I looked at each other. Could that be Atkins's voice which we heard? Indeed it was; and the next minute the man himself appeared, beaming with happiness, and tenderly supporting his wife. Pale and dishevelled, staggering slightly as she walked, she was but the wreck of her former self. Her husband laid her on a divan and, kneeling down beside her, murmured indistinguishable words of remorse and love. She lay quite still, her eyes closed, her breath coming in short gasps. I rushed off for some brandy, which I forced down her throat. That revived her, and she looked about her. When her eyes fell on the detective, she cried aloud and tried to struggle to her feet, but her husband put his arm around her and pulled her down again.

"Don't be afraid of him. He's all right."

"Really?"

She seemed but half reassured.

"You can trust me, I promise you," said the detective. "We are all quite sure you had nothing to do with the man's death. Only we must find out who he was, and when and how he left you. If you will tell us all that occurred, it may help us to discover the criminal."

"Did you know, Larrie, that the man came to the building to see me?"

Atkins nodded.

"And you are not angry?"

"No, indeed! Tell us all about it."

"Oh, I will, I will! I could never be real happy with a secret between us." She paused a moment. "Well, his name was Allan Brown, and years and years ago, when I was nothing but a silly girl, I fancied myself in love with him, and—and—I married him."

Atkins started back, and I feared for a moment that he would say or do

127

something which neither of them would ever be able to forget. But the past two days had taught him a lesson; the agony he had been through was still fresh in his mind; so, after a short struggle with himself, he took his wife's hand in his, and gently pressed it. The pretty blush, the happy smile, the evident relief with which she looked at him must have amply repaid him for his self-control.

"He treated me just shamefully," she continued, "and after three weeks of perfect misery, I left him. Pa at once began proceedings for a divorce, and, as Allan didn't contest it, it was granted me very shortly. I resumed my maiden name, and went back to live with my father. My experience of married life had been so terrible that I couldn't bear ever to think or speak of it. Years went by without anything occurring to remind me of my former husband, and I had almost succeeded in forgetting that there was such a person, when I met you, Larrie. The idea of marrying again had always been so abhorrent to me that I did not at first realise where we were drifting to, and you were such an impetuous wooer that I found myself engaged to you without having had any previous intention of becoming so. Of course, I ought then to have told you that I had been married before; there was nothing disgraceful in the fact, and you had a right to know it. Only, somehow, I just couldn't bear to let the memory of that hateful experience sully my new happiness, even for a moment; so I kept putting off telling you from day to day till the time went by when I could have done so, easily and naturally. At last, I said to myself: Why need Larrie ever know? Only a few of my old friends heard of my unfortunate marriage, and they were little likely ever to refer to the fact before you. It was even doubtful if you ever would meet any of them, as we were to live in New York. So I decided to hold my tongue. And all went well till one morning, a little over a fortnight ago. I was walking carelessly down Broadway, stopping occasionally to look in at some shop window, when a man suddenly halted in front of me. It was Allan Brown. I knew him at once, although he had altered very much for the worse. I remembered him a tall, athletic young man with fine, clear-cut features and a ruddy brown complexion. He was always so fussy about his clothes, that we used to call him 'Wales.' And now his coat was unbrushed, his boots were unblackened. He had grown fat; his features had become bloated, and his skin had a pasty, unhealthy look. I was so taken aback at his suddenly appearing like a ghost from my dead past, that I stood perfectly still for a minute. Then, as I realised the full extent of his impudence in daring to stop me, I tried to brush past him.

"'Not so fast, my dear, not so fast; surely a husband and wife, meeting after such a long separation, should at least exchange a few words before drifting apart again.'

"'You are no husband of mine,' I cried.

"'Really,' he exclaimed, lifting his eyebrows carelessly; 'since when have I ceased to be your husband, I should like to know?'

"That just took my breath away.

"'For ten years, thank God,' said I.

"'Well, it's always good to thank God,' and his wicked eyes smiled maliciously at me; 'only in this case he is receiving what he has not earned.'

"'What do you mean?' I asked.

"'That I have never ceased to be your husband, my dear.'

"'It's a lie, it's a lie!' I cried, but my knees began to tremble; 'I've been divorced from you for the last ten years, and don't you dare to pretend you don't know it.'

"'I needn't pretend at all, as it happens, for this is the first I ever have heard of it; and so, my dear wife, be very careful not to make another man happy on the strength of that divorce, for if you do, you may find yourself in a very awkward position, to say the least of it.'

"I looked at him. His manner had all the quiet assurance I remembered so well. Could what he said be true? Was it possible that my divorce was not legal? Father had said it was all right, but he might be mistaken, and, in that case, what should I do? My perturbation must have been written very plainly on my face, for, after watching me a minute in silence, he continued. 'Ah, I see that is what you have done—and who is my unlucky successor, if I may ask?'

"Now, I knew that he was capable of any deviltry, and, if he found out that I had married again, it would be just like him to go to you, and make a scene, just for the pleasure of annoying us. Besides, as I had not told you of my first marriage, it would be dreadful if you should hear of it from Allan Brown, of all people. You would never forgive me in that case, I felt sure. So I lifted my head; 'I have no husband,' said I.

"But he only smiled sarcastically at me, as he calmly lit a cigarette.

"'Prevarication, my dear lady, is evidently not your forte. Out with it. What is the name of the unhappy man? I only call him unhappy (*bien entendu*) because he is about to lose you.'

"'I'm not married,' I repeated.

"'I know you are married, and I mean to find out who to, if I have to follow you all day.'

"I had been walking rapidly along, hoping to shake him off, but he had persistently kept pace with me. Now I stopped. A policeman was coming towards us. In my desperation, I decided to ask him to arrest Allan for annoying me. The latter guessed my intention, and said: 'Oh, no; I wouldn't do that; I should inform him of the fact that you are my wife—an honour you seem hardly to appreciate, by the way—and you would have to accompany me to the police station, where our conflicting stories would no doubt arouse much interest, and probably be considered worthy of head-lines in the evening papers. Do you think the man you are now living with would enjoy your acquiring notoriety in such a way? Eh?'

"'Well,' I cried, 'what is it you want?'

"'The opportunity of seeing you again, that is all; you must acknowledge that I am very moderate in my demands. I do not brutally insist on my rights.'

"'But why—why do you wish to see me again?' I asked.

"'You are surprised that I should want to see my wife again? Really, you are so—so modern.'

"'Don't talk nonsense,' I said (for all this fooling made me mad). 'What do you want? Tell me at once.'

"'Really, my dear lady, since you are so insistent, I will be quite frank with you; I really don't know. I am enjoying this meeting extremely, and I think another may afford me equal pleasure.'

"'You devil!'

"'You never did appreciate me. Well, are you going to tell me what you now call yourself, or are we going to continue walking about together all day?'

"'I am Mrs. Henry Smith,' I said, at last.

"'H'm! Smith—not an unusual name, is it? Not much of an improvement on Brown, eh? And your address?'

"'The Waldorf,' I answered, naming the first place that came into my head.

"'How convenient! I am staying there also; so, instead of discussing our little differences in the street, let us drive back to the hotel at once,' and, before I realised what he was doing, he had hailed a cab. I started back.

"'Don't make a scene in public,' he commanded, and his manner became suddenly so fierce that I was fairly frightened, and obeyed him automatically. A moment later I was being driven rapidly up town.

"'I don't live at the Waldorf,' I at last acknowledged, as we were nearing

130

Thirty-third street.

"'Of course not, and your name isn't Smith; I know that; but where shall I tell the coachman to drive to?'

"There was no help for it; I had to give my real address.

"'And now let us decide when I shall call on you. I don't mind selecting a time when my rival is out. You see, I am very accommodating—at present,' he added, significantly.

"What was I to do? I dared not refuse him. I knew you would be out of town the following evening, so agreed to see him then. He did not follow me into the Rosemere, as I was afraid he might, but drove quickly off. I wrote and telegraphed at once to Pa, asking him to make sure that my divorce was perfectly legal. I hoped that I might receive a reassuring answer before the time set for my interview with Brown, in which case I should simply refuse to receive him and confess to you my previous marriage as soon as you returned. Then I should have nothing more to dread from him. That day and the next, however, went by without a word from Father. I couldn't understand his silence. It confirmed my worst fears. As the time when I expected my tormentor drew near, I became more and more nervous. I feared and hoped I knew not what from this meeting. I told both my girls they might go out, as I did not wish them to know about my expected visitor, and then regretted I had left myself so unprotected. So I got out my Smith & Wesson, and carefully loaded it. I can shoot pretty straight, and Allan was quite aware of that fact, I am glad to say; so I felt happier. He was so very late for his appointment, that I had begun to hope he was not coming at all, when the door-bell rang. As soon as I had let him in I saw that he had been drinking. Strangely enough, that reassured me somewhat; I felt that I and my pistol stood a better chance of being able to manage him in that condition than when that fiendish brain of his was in proper working order. He no longer indulged in gibes and sarcasms, but this time did not hesitate to demand hush money.

"'What is your price?' I asked.

"'A thousand dollars.'

"Of course, I had no such sum, nor any way of obtaining it. I told him so.

"'What rot! Why, those rings you've got on are worth more than that.'

"'Those rings were given to me by my husband, and if I part with them he will insist on knowing what has become of them.'

"'I don't care about that,' he said, settling himself deeper into his chair; 'either you give me that money or I stay here till your lover returns.'

"I knew him to be capable of it.

"'Look here,' said I, 'I can't get you a thousand dollars, so that's all there is about it; but if you'll take some jewelry that Pa gave me, and which I know is worth about that, I'll give it you on condition that you sign a paper, saying that you have blackmailed me, and that your allegations are quite without foundation.'

"'I won't take your jewelry on any consideration,' he answered. 'What should I do with it? if I sold it I could only get a trifle of what it is worth, besides running the risk of being supposed to have stolen it. No, no, my lady; it must be cash down or no deal.'

"After a great deal of further altercation, he agreed to wait twenty-four hours for his money. I was to employ this respite in trying to sell my jewelry, but if by the following evening I had failed to raise a thousand dollars he swore he would sell my story to the newspapers. He told me that he had an appointment in Boston the next morning, and that he had not enough money to pay his expenses. So he made me give him all the cash there was in the house. Luckily, I had very little. Before leaving, he lurched into the dining-room and poured himself out a stiff drink of whiskey.

"'Now, mind that you have that money by to-morrow evening, do you hear? And don't think I shan't be back in time to keep my appointment with you, for I shall. Never miss a date with a pretty woman, even if she does happen to be your wife, is my motto,' and with that final shot he departed. As the elevator had stopped running, I told him he would have to walk down-stairs. I stood for a moment watching him reel from side to side, and I wondered at the time if he would ever get down without breaking his neck. Not that I cared much, I confess; and that was the last I saw of him alive. The next day was spent in trying to raise that thousand dollars. The pawn brokers offered me an absurdly small sum for my jewelry, and wanted all sorts of proof that it was really my property. I tried to borrow from an acquaintance (I have no friends in New York), but she refused, and intimated that your wife could not possibly be in need of money except for an illegitimate purpose. She was quite right, and I liked her no less for her distrust of me. At last I made up my mind that it was impossible to raise the sum he demanded, and returned home determined to brazen it out. Still, no news from Father. What could be the reason of his silence, I wondered; any answer would be better than no answer.

"I braced myself to meet Allan, hopeless but resigned. However, hour after hour went by and still no sign of him. When eleven o'clock struck without his having put in an appearance, I knew that a respite had been mercifully granted me. I was expecting you home very shortly, so thought I'd sit up for you.

However, the fatigue and excitement of the last few days proved too much for me, and I fell asleep on the sofa. I had been longing for you all day, and fully intended to tell you the dreadful news as soon as I saw you. But somehow or other, when at last you did arrive you seemed so distant and cold that I weakly put off my confession till a more favourable moment."

Atkins hung his head.

"The next morning, when there was still no news of my persecutor, I began to breathe more freely. I was told that there had been an accident in the building, but that Allan Brown was the victim never occurred to me. Imagine my horror and consternation when, on being shown the corpse, I recognised my first husband. A thousand wild conjectures as to the cause of his death flashed through my mind, and when I heard that he had been murdered I feared for one awful moment that you might have met him and killed him either in anger or self-defence. When I learned that the crime had been committed on Tuesday I was inexpressibly relieved. For on that day you had not even been in New York. My next anxiety was lest the fact that the dead man had come to the building to see me should become known. When asked if I recognised the corpse I lied instinctively, unthinkingly. It was a crazy thing for me to have done, for I should have been instantly detected if it had not been for the surprising coincidence that Greywood (that's his name, isn't it), who had also been in the building that evening, so closely resembled my visitor. But I knew nothing of this, and had no intention of casting suspicion on any one else when I so stoutly denied all knowledge of the man. The Coroner's cross-questioning terrified me, for I was sure he suspected me of knowing more than I cared to say. But when that ordeal was over, and I was again within my own four walls, I could feel nothing but extreme thankfulness that the evil genius of my life was removed from my path at last. My only remaining fear was lest I should be suspected of his death. I imagined that I was being shadowed, and fancied that a man was stationed in the flat above the Doctor's, who watched this house night and day. Was that so, Mr. Merritt?"

"Yes'm."

"As the days went by I only became more nervous. The mystery of the thing preyed on my mind. The thought that I must be living under the same roof with a murderer gave me the creeps. Therefore, you can understand what a relief the butler's arrest was to me. But my joy did not last long. I met you, Doctor, and you let out that Mr. Merritt did not believe the Frenchman guilty, but was sure that a young woman had killed Allan. These words revived all my fears for my own safety. I was convinced that my former relation to the murdered man had been discovered, and that I should be accused of his death.

I could not bring such disgrace on you, Larrie, so determined to fly if possible before I was arrested. As you know, I left the house in the middle of the night, and I hid under a stoop in a neighbouring side-street till morning. All day long I wandered aimlessly about. I didn't dare to leave the city, for I was sure the trains would be watched. I daresn't go to a hotel without luggage. Towards evening I got desperate. Seeing a respectable-looking woman toiling along, with a baby on one arm and a parcel in the other, I stopped her. I begged her to tell me of some quiet place where I could spend the night. Having assured her that I was not unprovided with money, she gladly consented to take me to her own home. All she had to offer was a sofa, but, my! how glad I was to lie down at all. But the heat, the smell, the shouting and cursing of drunken brutes, prevented me from sleeping, and this morning I felt so ill I thought I should die. The desire to look once more at the house where I had been so happy grew stronger and stronger. At last I couldn't resist it. So I came, although I knew all the time I should be caught."

"And were you sorry to be caught?" asked her husband.

"No—o—," she answered, as she looked at the detective, apprehensively. "If I'm not to be imprisoned."

"Pray reassure yourself on that score, madam. The worst that will happen to you is that you will have to repeat part of your story at the inquest. No one can suspect you of having killed the man. The body must have been hidden somewhere for twenty-four hours, and in your apartment there is no place you could have done this, except possibly in the small coat closet under the stairs. But your waitress swears that she cleaned that very closet on the morning after the murder. Neither were you able as far as I can see to procure a key to the vacant apartment. No, madam, you will have absolutely no difficulty in clearing yourself."

"But the disgrace—the publicity——"

"There is no disgrace and hang the publicity," exclaimed Atkins.

"You forgive me?"

Atkins kissed her hand.

"But, darling, that divorce?" he asked, under his breath.

"Oh, I heard from Pa about a week ago. He had been travelling about and hadn't had his mail forwarded. That was the reason why I had had no answer to my numerous telegrams and letters. He says, however, that my divorce is O. K., so you can't get rid of me after all."

CHAPTER XVIII

THE TRUTH OF THE WHOLE MATTER

T HE Atkinses had departed, and Merritt and I were again alone.

"Well," I exclaimed, "the Rosemere mystery doesn't seem any nearer to being solved, does it?"

"You ought to be satisfied with knowing that your friend, Mrs. Atkins, is exonerated."

"Of that I am heartily glad; but who can the criminal be?"

The detective shrugged his shoulders.

"You don't know?" I asked.

"Haven't an idea," he answered.

"But what about that pretty criminal you've been talking so much about?"

"Well, Doctor, to tell you the truth this case has proved one too many for me. You see," he went on, settling himself more comfortably in his chair, "there isn't enough evidence against any one to warrant our holding them an hour. Mrs. Atkins knew the man and had a motive for killing him, but had no place in which to secrete the body, nor did she make any effort to obtain that key. Against Argot the case is stronger. One of the greatest objections to the theory that it was he who murdered Brown is that, as far as we can find out, the man was a perfect stranger to him. But as he did not know his wife's lover by sight, it seems to me not impossible that he may have mistaken Brown for the latter, and thought that in killing him he was avenging his honour. The Frenchman is also one of the few persons who could have abstracted the key of the vacant apartment. On the other hand, it would have been impossible for him to have either secreted or disposed of the body without his wife's knowledge. And unless Madame Argot is an actress and a liar of very unusual talent, I am willing to swear that she knew and knows nothing of the crime!"

"I am sure of it," I assented.

"Furthermore, I can think of no way by which Argot could have run across Brown. He would naturally follow the man whom he believed to be his wife's lover, and not only did Madame Argot tell you that her husband ran out the back way in pursuit of her cousin, but that seems to me the thing which he would most likely do. And yet, having left by that door, he could not possibly have got into the house again unperceived. Therefore, I cannot imagine how he could have met Allan Brown. No, there is really not a scrap of real evidence against the Frenchman. Now, there remains Miss Derwent. She could easily have obtained the key; she could also have hidden the body. But there is absolutely nothing to connect her with the murder, or the victim— nothing. And yet, Doctor, I have always believed that she knew more about this crime than she was willing to acknowledge, and I may as well tell you now that the reason I took such pains to inform Miss Derwent of Mrs. Atkins's plight, was that I thought that, rather than allow an innocent person to suffer, she would reveal the name of the true author of the crime. You see, I had exhausted every means of discovering her secret, without the least result. My only hope of doing so now lay with her. But my ruse failed. She has given no sign, although, for aught she knows, Mrs. Atkins may be languishing in a prison, or is being hunted from house to house or from city to city. I am therefore forced to believe that Miss Derwent's mysterious secret has absolutely nothing to do with the Rosemere murder."

"I have always been sure of it."

"But the fact remains that the man was killed. And yet every person who could by any possibility have committed the crime has practically been proved guiltless. I'm getting old." And he sighed deeply.

"So you have given the case up!"

"No, sirree. But I confess I'm not very hopeful. If I failed to pick up a clue while the scent was fresh, there ain't much chance of my doing it now. So I guess you've won your bet, Doctor," he went on, as he pulled a roll of bills out of his pocket.

"Certainly not. I bet that a man committed the crime, and that has not been proved, either."

"That's so! Well, good-day, Doctor. Hope I'll see you again. I tell you what, you should have been on the force." And so we parted.

He had hardly shut the door behind him, when my boy came in with a note. The handwriting was unknown to me. I tore the envelope open, and threw it down beside me. This is what I read:

DEAR DR. FORTESCUE,

I am in great trouble and beg you to come to me as soon as you possibly can.

Sincerely yours,
MAY DERWENT.

"Any answer, sir?"

"No." I should be there as soon as the messenger.

I was so dreadfully alarmed that I felt stunned for a moment. Pulling myself together, I started to my feet, when my eyes fell on the envelope, lying beside my plate. A large crest was emblazoned on its back. I stood spellbound, for that crest was, alas, not unfamiliar to me. I could not be mistaken —it was identical with the one engraved on the sleeve-link which had been found on the body of the murdered man. What did this similarity mean? Was it possible that the victim's real name was Derwent? That would account for the coincidence of the two Allans, and all I knew of one was equally applicable to the other. Merritt had told me that Brown was supposed to have been born a gentleman, and often posed as an Englishman of title. But if the corpse was indeed that of her brother, why had May not recognised it? No, the probabilities were, as the detective had said, that the crest meant nothing.

Still deeply perturbed, I hastened to the hotel. On giving my name I was at once ushered into the Derwent's private sitting-room. It was empty, but a moment later May appeared. She was excessively pale, and heavy dark rings encircled her eyes. I longed to take her in my arms, but all I dared to do was to detain her small hand in mine till after several efforts on her part to free herself—very gentle efforts, however—I finally relinquished it.

"It is kind of you to come so soon."

"You knew I would come the moment I received your message."

"I hoped so. All night long I have lain awake, praying for courage to make a confession, knowing all the time that if I do so it will break my mother's heart."

"Your mother's heart!" I repeated, bewildered.

"It must be done, it is right that it should be done—but I can't do it. I have, therefore, decided to tell you the whole story, and then you can repeat it to her very gently, very calmly, which I could not do. And you will remain to comfort her when I am gone, won't you?"

"Don't talk in this way," I commanded, forcibly possessing myself of her hands. "You are not going to die."

"Don't touch me," she entreated, tearing herself away from me. "You won't want to, when you know the truth. I have not only committed a dreadful crime, but have allowed an innocent person to suffer in my stead. I should have confessed to the detective yesterday that I knew Mrs. Atkins had not killed the man, because—because—I myself killed him."

I was so overcome with horror and surprise at hearing this confession, that for a moment I was paralysed.

"My poor darling," I exclaimed at last, "how did this accident occur?"

She had evidently expected me to express horror and indignation, and that I did not do so was such an unexpected relief, that the poor child burst into tears. This time she did not repulse me. When she had become a little calmer, she said:

"I am glad that there is one person at least who, hearing that admission, does not at once believe me guilty of a dreadful crime. Oh, I assure you, I swear to you, that I never meant to kill the—the—fellow." She shuddered.

"Of course you didn't. Tell me all about it, and let me see if I can't help you in some way."

A faint gleam of hope shot across her face.

"It is a long story," she began. "You remember that I told the Coroner about a certain gentleman who called on me on that fatal Tuesday evening?"

"Yes."

"Well, that was all true. Mr. Greywood (for, of course, you now know that that was my visitor's name) and I quarrelled (no matter why), and we parted in anger. This is no news to you. What happened later is what I have tried so hard to conceal. Mr. Greywood had hardly left when I was startled by a violent ringing at the door-bell. Thinking that it was my late visitor who had returned, to apologise, probably, I hurried to the door, and incautiously opened it. In the dim light, the man before me resembled Mr. Greywood so closely that I did not doubt that it was he, and moved aside to allow him to enter. As he did so, he pushed roughly against me. I stared at him in astonishment, and to my horror, discovered that I was face to face with a perfect stranger. The fellow banged the door behind him, and stood with his back against it. He was mumbling something I couldn't catch, and his head rolled alarmingly from side to side. That the man was insane was the only thing that occurred to me, and as I realised that I was locked into an apartment with a lunatic, I became panic-stricken, and lost my head. Instead of making a dash for the upper floor, where I could either have barricaded myself into one of the bed rooms, or perhaps have managed to escape by the back stairs, I stupidly ran into the drawing-room, which is only shut off from the hall by portières, and has no other outlet. The brute, of course, followed me, and stood in the door way, barring my exit. I was caught like a rat in a trap. He lurched in my direction, muttering imprecations. His speech was so thick that I could only understand a word here and there. I made out, however, that he wished me to give him something that night, which, he said, I had promised to let him have the next day. As he staggered toward me, I uttered a piercing shriek, but even as I did so, I knew that there was little or no chance of anybody's hearing me. The building was almost empty, and the street at that hour practically deserted.

"In the middle of our room opposite the fire place, stands a large sofa. When his eyes fell upon that he paused a minute. 'Perhaps I'll go to bed,' I heard him say, and forthwith he proceeded to take off his coat and waistcoat. Meanwhile, I was cowering near the window. As he had apparently forgotten me, I began to hope that I might possibly succeed in creeping past him unobserved. But, unfortunately, as I was attempting to do so, my skirt caught in something, and I fell forward on my hands and knees. The noise attracted his attention, and he paused in his undressing to look at me. I sprang to my feet. We stared at each other for a few seconds, and I thought I saw a ray of comprehension come into his dull eyes. 'I don't think I ever met this lady before,' he mumbled.

"He tried to pull himself together, and made me an awkward bow. I stood perfectly still. The wretch smiled horridly at me. Of course, I now see that I ought to have humoured him, instead of which I was injudicious enough to meet his advances with a fierce scowl. That apparently infuriated the fellow, for he sprang towards me, cursing loudly. I had not thought him capable of such agility, so was unprepared for the attack. He caught my wrist. I tried to wrench it from him, but he was very strong, and I soon realised that I was quite powerless in his grasp. Yet I would not give in, but continued to struggle fiercely. Oh, it was too awful!"

The unfortunate girl paused a moment and covered her face with her hands, as if she were trying to shut out the memory of that terrible scene.

"At last the end came. He had got me into a corner. Escape was impossible. My back was against the wall, and in front of me towered the wretch, his hands on my shoulders, his poisoned breath blowing into my face. Now, remember, before you blame me for what followed, that I was perfectly desperate. As I glanced frantically around, hoping against hope to find some way out of my awful situation, my eyes fell upon a hat-pin, which lay on a table by my side, well within reach of my right hand. It was sticking in my hat, which I had carelessly thrown down there when I came in from dinner a few hours before. It may be that its design, which was that of a dagger, suggested my putting it to the use I did. I don't know. At any rate, I seized it, and managed to get it in between me and my assailant, with its sharp point pressing against his chest. By this time I had become convinced that the man was simply intoxicated, and, hoping to frighten him, I cried: 'Let me go. If you don't, I will kill you.' Yes, I said that; I acknowledge it. But I had no real intention of doing such a thing. I didn't even dream that I held in my hand a weapon. What happened then I don't quite know. Whether he tripped over something, or whether he was so drunk that he lost his balance, I can't tell. At all events, he fell heavily against me. If I had not been braced against the wall he certainly would have knocked me down. As it was, I was stunned for a minute. Recovering myself, I pushed him from me with all my strength. He reeled back, staggered a few steps, and then, to my surprise, fell flat upon the floor. As I stood staring at him, too frightened still to take advantage of this opportunity to escape, I heard a queer rattling in his throat. What could be the matter, I wondered, and what was that sticking out of his shirt, right over his heart? Could it be my hat-pin? I looked down at my hands; they were empty. Slowly the truth dawned upon me. I rushed to his side, looked into his glazing eyes, saw the purple fade from his face, and a greenish hue creep into its place. As the full horror of my position was borne in upon me, I thought I should go mad. I seized the pin and tried to drag it out, actuated by an unreasoning hope that if I could only extract it from the wound the man might even yet revive. But my hands must have been paralysed with fear, for, although I tugged and tugged, I failed to move it. At last, after an especially violent effort, I succeeded in pulling it out, but unfortunately in doing so the head broke off. I peered again at the man. Still no sign of life, but I could not, would not believe the worst. Overcoming my horror of the fellow, I bent down and shook his arm. I shall never forget the sensation it gave me to touch him. I could doubt the awful truth no longer: the man was dead, and I had killed him. Then for a time I lost consciousness. Unfortunately I am young and strong, and soon revived. When I did so I found myself lying on the floor not a foot away from that horrible thing that had so lately been a man. I feared him as much dead as alive, and, staggering to my feet, I fled from the room. Oh, the darkness, the frightful darkness which confronted me everywhere! In my terror of it I rushed hither and thither, leaving the electric light shining in my wake. I felt I must know, that I must be able to see, that he, who would never stir again, was not still following me. Stumbling up stairs in my haste, I locked myself into my bedroom. There I tried to think, but all I could do was to crouch, trembling, behind the door, listening for I knew not what. Several times I thought I heard footsteps stealing softly up the stairs.

"At last, the day dawned and brought with it comparative calm. I was now able to consider my position. It was, indeed, a desperate one. What should I do? Whom could I appeal to? My mother? Another helpless woman—never! Then Mr. Norman occurred to me. I felt I could rely on him. He would save me if any one could. I decided to go to him as soon as possible. I knew that I must be most careful not to do anything which might arouse suspicion. I, therefore, made up my mind not to leave the house before half-past seven at the earliest. I could then be supposed to be going out to breakfast. The hours crept wearily by. I watched the hot, angry sun rise superbly above the horizon, and fancied that it glared contemptuously down on my ruined life. To make matters worse, my watch had stopped, and I had to guess at the time by the various signs of reawakening which I could observe in the street beneath me. At last I decided that I might safely venture forth. Burning with impatience to be gone, I turned towards the door. Suddenly I remembered that my hat still lay in the room below. I started back, trembling in every limb. Never, never should I have the courage to enter there alone. Then I thought of the alternative. Summoning the police—the awful publicity, a prison cell and perhaps finally—no, no, I couldn't face that. Anything rather than that. No one will ever know how I felt as I slowly unlocked my door. My teeth chattered notwithstanding the heat, and half-fainting with terror I staggered down-stairs. Everywhere the lights still glowed feebly—sickly reminders of the horrors of the night. I don't remember how I got into the drawing-room, but the scene that greeted my eyes there can never be erased from my memory. The blazing August sun shone fiercely down on the disordered room, mercilessly disclosing the havoc which the recent struggle had wrought. In the midst of this confusion, that ghastly, silent object lay, gaping at the new day. His sightless eyes seemed to stare reproachfully at me. I turned quickly away. This was no time for weakness. If I indulged my fears I should be unable to accomplish what I had to do. Fixing my eyes on the thing I was in search of, I walked steadily past the corpse, but, having once seized what I had come for, I rushed frantically from the room and the apartment. The heavy outer door securely fastened behind me, made a sufficiently formidable barrier between the dead and myself to give me a sense of comparative safety. Still panting with excitement, I paused a moment on the landing. Reminding myself of how important it was that nothing about me should excite remark, I put on my hat and adjusted my thick veil with the utmost care, although my stiff, shaking fingers were hardly able to perform their task. Then, summoning up all my self-control I was ready to face the world again."

She stopped, and sank back exhausted.

"Go on," I begged; "what did you do then?"

"I knew that if Mr. Norman was in town at all, he would be at his father's house," May continued, more quietly.

"Hailing a cab, I drove directly there. You can imagine in what an overwrought state I was when I tell you that the idea that I was doing anything unusual never occurred to me. I rang the bell and asked for Mr. Stuart Norman without the least embarrassment. The butler's look of surprise and his evident unwillingness to admit me, recalled me a little to my senses. But even when I saw how my conduct must strike others, I did not turn back, and I finally persuaded the man to call his master. The latter hurried from the breakfast table to see who the mysterious and importunate female might be who had come knocking so early at his door. Notwithstanding my veil, he recognised me at once. Ushering me into a small reception room he closed the door behind him; then turning towards me he took me by the hand and, gently leading me to a sofa, begged me to tell him what had happened. I told my dreadful story as briefly as possible. You can imagine with what horror he listened. Strangely enough, I remained perfectly calm. I was astonished at my own callousness, but at the moment I felt as if all that had occurred was nothing but a hideous nightmare, from which I had happily awakened. When I had finished, Mr. Norman did not speak for some time, but paced up and down the room with ill-concealed agitation. Trying to appear calm, he again sat down beside me.

"'I have come to the conclusion that the only thing for you to do is to return at once to the Rosemere,' he said at last. This suggestion at once dispelled the numbness which had come over me, and the painful fluttering of my heart convinced me that the power of suffering had, alas, not left me. I first thought that he intended me to go back alone, but that I knew I could *not* do. He soon reassured me on that point, however, and promised that as long as I needed him, or wanted him, he would never desert me. He seemed to understand intuitively how I shrank from returning to the scene of the tragedy, and I felt sure he would not urge me to do so if he did not think it absolutely necessary. He pointed out that the body must be removed from our apartment as soon as possible. Where to put it was the question. We thought of various places, none of which seemed practicable, till I remembered the vacant suite on our landing. As soon as I told him of it, and that at present painters and paper-hangers were working there, he decided that we could never find a more convenient spot, or one where the discovery of the dead man was so little likely to compromise any one. How Mr. Norman was to get into our apartment was the next question. For obvious reasons he could not do so openly. At last, he hit on the idea of disguising himself as a tradesman. He suggested that we should both enter the building at the same time, I by the front, and he by the back door. I was then to let him in through the kitchen, which could easily be done without anybody's being the wiser. This seemed the most feasible plan, and I agreed to it. It would take him only a few minutes to dress, he assured me, but while I was waiting he begged me to have some breakfast. I told him that it would be impossible for me to eat, but he insisted. As it was most important that the servants should not recognise me, he took me to a quiet restaurant round the corner. There he ordered an ample breakfast, and stayed (notwithstanding my protests) till he satisfied himself that I had done full justice to it. He was gone an incredibly short time, and when he did return I had some difficulty in recognising him, so faultless, to my inexperienced eyes, did his get-up appear. He did not enter the restaurant, but lounged outside, chewing a straw with apparent carelessness. That straw was a very neat touch, for it permitted him to distort his mouth without exciting remark. A battered straw hat, drawn well over his eyes, a large apron, and a market-basket completed the transformation. Even if he had come face to face with a party of friends, I doubt if they would have known him. For who could suspect a man like Mr. Norman of masquerading as a tradesman? People would therefore be inclined to attribute any likeness they observed to an accidental resemblance."

So he was the tradesman I had seen leaving the Rosemere! I felt a terrible pang of jealousy, but managed to ask: "What did his servants think at seeing their master go out in such costume?"

"Later on, he told me that he had been able to leave the house unperceived," she replied; "at least, he thought so, as all the servants happened to be at breakfast. He had crept softly up-stairs, put on an old suit and hat, both of which had suffered shipwreck; then, with infinite precautions, he had stolen into the butler's pantry, seized an apron, stuffed it inside his coat, which he buttoned over it, and, after watching till the street was clear, slipped quietly out. When he turned the corner, and fancied himself unobserved, he pulled out the apron and tied it on. Then, walking boldly into Bloomingdale's, he purchased a market-basket, into which, with great forethought, he put a few needful groceries. All this, as I said before, he told me later. At the time, I left the restaurant without even glancing in his direction. We boarded the same car, but sat as far apart as possible. All went off as we had arranged, and half an hour later I had let him into our kitchen without having aroused anybody's suspicions." She paused a moment.

"Mr. Norman went at once into the room where the body lay," she continued. "He went alone, as I dared not follow him. When he came out he told me that he had pulled down all the shades, as, owing to the intense heat, he feared that some one might be tempted to climb to the opposite roof, in which case a chance look would lead to the discovery of my ghastly secret. The quiet and business-like way in which he talked of our situation was most comforting, and I was surprised to find myself calmly discussing the different means of obtaining possession of the key to the vacant apartment. This must be my task, as he could not go outside the door, for fear of being seen. So I stole out on the landing to reconnoitre. To my joy, I saw the key sticking in the lock. When Mr. Norman heard of this piece of good luck, it did not take him long to decide on a plan of action. Hastily scribbling a few lines to his butler, he gave them to me. He then told me to go out again and ring for the elevator. While waiting for it to come, I was to saunter casually to the threshold of the adjoining flat, and, leaning on the door-knob, quietly abstract the key. Should any one notice me, my curiosity would be a sufficient excuse for my presence. Having got the key and enclosed it in the envelope he had given me, I was to hurry to a district messenger office (taking care to select one where I was not likely to be known), send the note, and there await the answer, which would be addressed to Miss Elizabeth Wright. In this note he gave orders to have the key duplicated as quickly and secretly as possible. Mr. Norman thought that the butler, who was a man of great discretion, and had been with the family for many years, could be entrusted with this delicate mission, but anyhow we had to risk it as the only alternative (my going to a locksmith myself) was not to be thought of. The police would be sure to make inquiries of all such people, and if they discovered that a girl answering to my description had been to them on such an errand, it would fasten suspicion upon me and prove a perhaps fatal clue. I thought his plan most ingenious, and promised to follow his instructions to the letter. I had no difficulty in obtaining the key, although my extreme nervousness made me so awkward that I almost dropped it at the critical moment. After that everything else was easy. It seemed, however, an interminable time before I at last held both keys in my hand. I flew back to the Rosemere. Impatience lent wings to my feet. But here a disappointment awaited me. On stepping out of the elevator, I found the hall full of workmen, noisily eating their luncheons. There was no help for it—I must postpone returning the key till later. This agitated me very much, as I feared every moment that its absence would be discovered. Mr. Norman, however, took the delay much more philosophically than I did, and reassured me somewhat by saying that he did not believe any one would think of the key till evening. Still, as it was advisable to run as few risks as possible, I decided to make another attempt as soon as the men returned to their work. Peeping through a crack of our door, I waited till the coast was clear before venturing out. After ringing the elevator bell, I walked boldly forward, and had already stretched out my hand towards the key-hole, when a queer grating noise made me pause. A tell-tale boot was thrust suddenly out, and to my horror I discovered that a man was standing directly behind the door, busily scraping off the old paint. The narrowness of my escape made me feel quite faint. Another moment and the click of the lock would have betrayed me, and then—but I could not indulge in such conjectures. Swallowing my disappointment, I got into the lift. There was no help for it; I dared not try again till later in the day. In the meantime, I decided to do some shopping, as I wanted to be able to give that as an excuse for my prolonged stay in town. After spending several hours in this way, I concluded that I might again make an effort to replace the key, and this time I was successful, for although I met one of the workmen, yet I am sure he had not noticed that I had been fumbling with the lock. I found Mr. Norman, on my return, as calm and cheerful as ever. He urged me not to stay in the apartment, and although I felt ashamed to leave him to face the situation alone, yet the place was so dreadful to me that I yielded to my fears and his entreaties, and went out again and wandered aimlessly about till it grew so dark that I no longer dared to remain out alone. It is impossible for me to describe the ensuing evening. We sat together in the kitchen, as being the spot farthest from the scene of the tragedy. At first we tried to talk, but as the hours crept by, we grew more and more taciturn. We had decided that at two o'clock we would attempt our gruesome task, for that is the time when the world sleeps most soundly. Mr. Norman suggested that I should muffle myself up as much as possible, so that in case we were discovered, I might yet escape recognition, or, what would be even better, observation. I therefore put on a dark shirtwaist I found hanging in my closet, drew on a pair of black gloves to prevent my hands attracting attention, and tied up my hair in a black veil, which I could pull down over my face in case of emergency. Two o'clock at last struck. We immediately— but why linger over the gruesome details of what occurred during the next fifteen minutes? Fortunately, no one surprised us as we staggered across the landing with our burden, and we managed to get back to the shelter of our four walls unobserved. As we stood for a moment in the hall congratulating ourselves on having got rid of the body so successfully, I noticed a long, glittering object lying at my feet. Bending down, I picked it up. It was the fatal hat-pin. I dropped it with a shudder. Mr. Norman asked me what it was. I told him. He picked it up again and examined it closely. 'Where is the head of this pin?' he asked. I had no idea. I remembered that it had broken off in my hand as I wrenched it out of the body, and I thought that in all probability it still lay somewhere in the drawing-room, unless it had been carried elsewhere by the same chance which had swept its other part into the hall. Mr. Norman looked very grave when he heard of this loss, and said he would look for it immediately. He insisted, however, on my going to my room and trying to get some sleep. But sleep was, of course, out of the question, and at six o'clock I crept down stairs to bid my kind friend good-bye. We had concluded that at that hour he could easily leave the building unobserved.

"I had to wait till later, and just as I thought the time for my release had come the janitor brought me a request, a command rather, from the Coroner, to the effect that I was to remain on the premises till he had seen me. If McGorry had not been so excited himself he must have noticed my agitation, for I jumped at once to the conclusion that my secret was discovered. Luckily, I had time enough before I was finally called to regain my self-possession, and to decide how I had better behave so as to dissipate suspicion, even if it had already fastened upon me. I knew that to show too much emotion would be fatal. I must try and prove to them that I was not particularly affected by the sight of the corpse, and yet must be careful not to go to the other extreme and appear callous. How could I do this? Had I enough self-control to risk raising my veil when I entered the room where the dead man lay? If I did this and showed a calm, grave face, I believed it would go far towards establishing my innocence in the minds of those who would be watching me. And I think I *did* hide my agitation till the detective asked me a question I was quite unprepared for."

"You did, indeed," I assured her.

"When the ordeal was at last over, and Mr. Merritt had handed me into a cab, I really thought that I had allayed all suspicion. On arriving at Thirty-fourth Street Ferry, I was detained by a collision which had occurred between two vehicles, and as I was afraid of missing my train I jumped out in the middle of the street. As I was paying my fare, another hansom dashed up and I saw the man who was in it making desperate efforts to attract the driver's attention. Having at last succeeded in doing so, the horse was pulled up on its haunches and the man sprang out, knocking against me as he did so. He apologised profusely, and I noticed that he was an insignificant-looking person, a gentleman's servant, perhaps, and thought no more about him. I did not see him on the ferry, but after I had taken my seat in the cars I turned around and saw that he was sitting almost directly behind me. It then occurred to me that I ought to have telegraphed to my mother and asked her to send the carriage to meet me. I looked at my watch. The train would not start for six minutes. I got off and hurried towards the telegraph office, but, catching sight of the station clock, I saw that my watch had been slow and that I had barely time to regain my seat. Turning abruptly around, I almost ran into a man's arms. I started back and recognised, to my surprise, the same fellow I had already noticed twice before. I then made up my mind that he was following me. I jumped on to the last car and stood outside on the platform. A moment later the man appeared. Seeing me he hurried forward, but I had found out what I wanted to know.

"I walked back to my seat, outwardly calm, but inwardly a prey to the most dreadful emotions. What could I do? Nothing. On arriving at my destination the fellow also alighted, and as I drove home I felt he was still following me. After that, knowing that I was being shadowed, I had not a moment's peace. I dared not go beyond the gate. I dared not roam around the garden. I hardly knew what I feared, for of course they could have arrested me as easily in the house as outside. At last, I could bear the strain no longer and sent for Mr. Norman. His presence gave me a wonderful sense of security, and as I did not see my persecutor for several days, I really began to hope that the Rosemere tragedy would always remain a mystery, when, picking up the paper one morning, I read that a wretched Frenchman was suspected of the—the death. Of course, there was nothing else for me to do; I must give myself up. Then, you, Doctor, suggested that it might not be necessary, after all—oh, you gave that advice quite unconsciously. I knew that. But when you told me that the man, Argot, was hopelessly insane, and would in any case spend the rest of his days in a lunatic asylum, I wondered if the sacrifice of my life were indeed demanded. At any rate I felt I must go to New York so as to be on hand in case something unexpected occurred, and to watch developments. You can now understand why I begged you so hard to persuade Mamma to bring me here. When I had at last induced you all to let me come, I went out for a walk and was terribly frightened by a tramp whom I mistook for a detective. On reaching New York, I found there was nothing to be done here, and yet I have felt much more calm than I did in the country. Then, yesterday, I met Mr. Merritt, who told me that Mrs. Atkins was suspected, and had fled from her home in consequence. I might hold my tongue where a poor mad creature was concerned, whom my confession could not benefit, but in this case it was not to be thought of. I had a great many last things to attend to, so I decided not to give myself up till to-day. That is the end of my story."

And it is very nearly the end of mine. I easily persuaded May that to make her confession public would do no good to any one. When the inquest was held Mrs. Atkins told what she knew of the deceased, and although several people considered that her conduct had been suspicious, yet no one, I think, questioned that the verdict that Allan Brown met his death "by a person or persons unknown," was the only one which could have been rendered. I have never really learned whether the name of the Rosemere victim was Derwent or Brown. As May had not seen her brother since he left his home many years before as a beardless boy, it is quite possible that her failure to recognise him was simply due to the great change which dissipation, as well as years, had wrought in him. However, as young Derwent was never again heard of, I have always believed that it is he who lies in some unnamed grave in the potter's field. But that his fate may never become known to his mother and sister, is my most ardent wish.

Years have passed since these occurrences took place, and May Derwent is, I am glad to say, May Derwent no longer.

From time to time I see Merritt, but as he will talk of nothing but the Rosemere murder, I avoid him as much as possible. I am sure that, although he has never been able to discover a single damaging fact against my wife, yet his detective instinct tells him that she alone could solve, if she wanted to, the mystery of "The House Opposite."